BLIND RAGE

By Adam Zorzi

BLIND RAGE

Limitless Publishing, LLC
Kailua, HI 96734
www.limitlesspublishing.com

Formatting: Limitless Publishing

ISBN-13: 978-1-64034-141-8
ISBN-10: 1-64034-141-2

Dedication

Ai fantasmi di Richmond

CHAPTER ONE

May

"Security was tight at the Dinwiddie County Circuit Court today, as the man known as the Psycho Killer was sentenced. He was found guilty of second-degree murder in the death of a patient in the Forensic Unit of Virginia Commonwealth Psychiatric Hospital in Petersburg eighteen months ago," said a young woman in an ill-fitting navy blue suit, yellow blouse, and mid-heeled pumps.

"The Psycho Killer was deemed an especially high security risk. Precautions for his appearance included shackling his legs and arms to a wheelchair into which he was strapped, removing his shoes, and forcing him to wear a spit guard and blindfold."

"He was accompanied by eight armed sheriff's deputies—two each in the front, back, and on both sides of the wheelchair. All deputies remained at a distance of more than an arm's length to prevent the Psycho Killer from seizing one of their weapons and firing."

Fuzzy black and white video showed an unidentifiable object on wheels surrounded by deputies rolling down a hall toward the courtroom.

"This guy never had a chance," Mark scoffed. He stood next to his associate Tom in front of the TV in his office with his arms folded across his chest.

"What do you mean?" Tom asked.

"He's called the Psycho Killer instead of his name, trussed up and blindfolded to make him look like Hannibal Lechter, and surrounded by eight armed guards. It would serve the county right if he grabbed a gun, tipped over the wheelchair, and started firing blindly. He, too, was a patient at Commonwealth Psych at the time. No one mentions that."

An aerial shot of the hospital campus appeared on the screen as the reporter continued.

"Commonwealth Psychiatric Hospital, established in 1869, has a long history of murders, hauntings, and paranormal sightings. The 167-bed forensic unit, which is the only one in the state, houses defendants who are awaiting competency hearings as well as those inmates found not guilty of crimes by reason of insanity, or NGRI."

"You sound…" Tom started.

"Quiet. I want to hear this," Mark said.

"…strangling nineteen-year-old Evan Cooper to death with his bare hands. The Psycho Killer was in the state forensic hospital awaiting a competency hearing for arson and the murder of two elderly women in Lynchburg. Mr. Cooper was at

Commonwealth Psychiatric Hospital to receive drug addiction treatment as his sentence for robbing a convenience store owner for cash to buy heroin."

Mark shouted at the TV. "Absurd. Why was this teenage drug addict in the same ward that houses the most violent inmates?" He put his hands on his hips and blew out a deep breath.

File footage of the jury filing out of the courthouse after the verdict was rendered streamed behind the reporter.

"The jury was out for just thirty minutes before reaching a guilty verdict. In an exclusive interview with one of the jurors who asked not to be named, this reporter was told that the primary evidence for a guilty verdict was a surveillance tape that showed the Psycho Killer entering the victim's room three times between ten-thirty and eleven o'clock that night. After the third visit, the lights went off in the victim's room."

"If there's surveillance video, shouldn't hospital security be watching that monitor to intervene?" Mark shouted.

"You're really wound tight about this," Tom observed.

"It makes the state and the justice system look incredibly stupid," Mark declared. Tom shrugged. That pissed Mark off, too. He hated that outsiders like Tom assumed southerners were inferior and incompetent. Worse, this kind of justice proved their point.

"Can't wait to hear the sentence," Mark said.

An exterior shot of the courthouse was shown.

"...sentenced to forty years, the maximum

penalty allowed by law. All of us hope this brings the Cooper family some closure. Back to you."

Tom headed back to his office. "Maybe you should handle the family's wrongful death suit against Commonwealth."

Mark clicked off the TV. "I may just do that."

***

Ghost Bella Davis had watched the same newscast. What a farce. That hospital should have been shut down decades ago. No accredited hospital would allow a murderer of questionable competency free rein in the same ward as a teenage drug addict. More importantly, the murderer was in proximity to Daniel. Her Daniel.

Six years earlier, she and Daniel were close to their goal of being together for eternity when he'd wavered and hurt her. She needed to teach him a lesson. She murdered his wife and framed him with the expectation that he would be remanded to Commonwealth Psychiatric for just three months. A deal was in place whereby he would then be declared competent to stand trial, his ferocious attorney Nina Lombardi would move to dismiss the charges, and the Commonwealth Attorney wouldn't object. The case would be dismissed. Daniel would be hers. They'd become eternal lovers.

In a rare miscalculation of Daniel's mental health, Bella watched helplessly as Daniel sank into catatonia for two years. Through her exhaustive efforts to find a specialist to treat catatonia, Bella found a pioneering neurologist who successfully brought Daniel back to the world. While Daniel worked to recover his physical and cognitive abilities at Commonwealth Psych, Bella gave Daniel a gift that she knew would make him happy and perhaps speed his recovery.

Bella arranged for Daniel to learn he and Bella had a daughter named LouLou who had been born in Paris and adopted by a couple in diplomatic service. By sheer happenstance, LouLou had not remained in Paris, the city of her birth, but lived in Richmond, where she worked as a DJ. This revelation made Daniel ecstatic, as Bella knew it would. He'd be on his way to health and happiness and a reunion with Bella.

Again, Bella's plan failed to bring Daniel comfort. Despite Bella's behind-the-scenes maneuvering to force LouLou to accept Daniel as her father, the stubborn, sickly woman refused. Daniel. Sweet, loving, kind Daniel who could've added so much to LouLou's life was kicked away. Naturally, her rejection only intensified Daniel's desire to be with LouLou. The sniveling LouLou made such a fuss that Daniel was sent back to Petersburg on a stalking charge.

Bella made sure LouLou paid for that. If Bella couldn't be with her lover, neither could LouLou. She snatched LouLou's lover Gregg from her by causing a car accident the day after Christmas. That stunt had been quite theatrical and fun. Dressed as an angel holding the manger child, Bella stood in the snow on the highway until a multi-vehicle pile-up occurred. Drivers swore they saw her standing serenely as she held the baby and swerved to avoid hitting her. She vanished. Witnesses spread the word that it was a miracle. Actually, Bella just made herself invisible and dumped the costume and doll in Monte Carlo, where she spent her holiday. Bella was pleased the location had become a shrine of sorts. She liked accolades.

More importantly, she'd dragged Greg out of LouLou's car and deposited him in Phuket. If he had any ghostly wits about him, he'd be able to make it back to LouLou. If not, too bad for them.

Daniel had just been released from a private hospital, but Bella intended to make sure that he'd never go to Commonwealth Psych again. She'd burn the bloody place down before she'd let that happen. Bella had a plan to make sure Commonwealth Psych wouldn't be around for much longer while she waited for Daniel to regain his physical strength. Daniel was working hard, and Bella understood that his rehab was difficult, but she was getting impatient. She wanted him well and with her for eternity.

CHAPTER TWO

September

Mark Hoffman sat alone in the back booth of the storied Beacon Bar and Grill after glad-handing his way through lawyers and politicians having drinks after work at the courthouse and state house Friday evening. When the House of Delegates was in a special session, as they were now, Richmond was filled with politicians from all the burgs of the state looking to score big graft, a juicy alliance, or a hot hooker. Mark wanted a steak and a scotch.

He was on his second scotch when a gorgeous blonde with stunning blue eyes in a beautifully tailored black suit took the seat across from him in the booth.

"Yes, please join me," he said, nodding to the seat.

"I don't take requests," Bella said in her mellifluous voice that could charm even the coldest heart. "Would you like me to leave?"

The waiter served Mark's steak and didn't glance

at his new companion.

"Do you want a menu?" Mark asked.

"No. I'm here to talk, but don't let your meal get cold. Please eat."

He did. Good table manners. Didn't talk to hear the sound of his voice. She liked that in a man.

He was smart to choose the rear booth. The front was hot, noisy, and loud. If a man wanted to be able to enjoy his food without someone spilling a drink on him, hitting on him, or sidling up to him, Mark had found the perfect spot. A bit of an outsider.

"Mark. Mr. Hoffman seems too formal since we'll be working together."

He took a sip of water. She could tell his mind was racing to place her or remember offering her a job. She sat quietly and let him work it out.

"On the Evan Cooper case," she prodded.

"I haven't taken it yet." He returned to his meal.

She laughed. That marvelous laugh that made most men weak. "Mark, we're not going to be able to work together if you lie to me. You have the retainer check in your jacket pocket. You didn't stop by the ATM to deposit it on the way here. The Coopers made only a nominal payment to start the proceedings and you'll be winning them a nice sum from the Commonwealth. Of course, it won't bring back their son, but it will represent a victory against the incompetent hospital administration that allowed him to be killed so brutally."

"Keep talking," he said as he continued to eat.

"You also have the complaint you were going to file with the court clerk, but you missed the deadline. Those doors lock at 4:59 pm. Don't worry.

There are changes that should be made. You don't want to amend the complaint. Messy. Amateurish. Not the way to present yourself."

"Who are you?" he asked after he'd finished and pushed his plate to the side.

"Someone interested in seeing that hellhole in Petersburg permanently shuttered."

"Spend time there?" He looked her directly in the eyes.

Good sign. He was up to a challenge and had a sense of humor. "Not me. Let's just call it in the interest of justice."

"Justice. Even a first-year law student knows that's the weakest legal argument." He finished his scotch, set the tumbler back on the table, and placed his linen napkin to the side of it.

"Yes," she said with a slight frown on her face, "but so many people believe it. Occasionally, they should get it. Keep up appearances for the legal machine."

He laughed. When he did, his eyes crinkled and he looked boyish. He was handsome. Dark hair, blue eyes, tan.

"What's in it for you?"

"A way to pass the time. I'm waiting for an opportunity that won't be available for another ten months or so." She was casual. She knew he'd cave, but she liked a bit of a chase.

"Are you even a lawyer?"

"Columbia Law. New York Bar. Supreme Court Bar." She slid out of the booth. "You'll want to make those changes to the complaint before filing." He looked down at the USB drive she'd placed on the dark wood table.

"What's your name?" he asked.

She was gone.

CHAPTER THREE

Mark looked up from his computer to see Bella seated in the white leather chair across from his glass desk. Her entrance had been completely silent.

"Genius," he said. "Why bother with state courts when we can go federal for civil rights violations. Faster. Smarter judges. More money."

"I thought you'd reconsider your strategy." Bella turned her attention to wardrobe. "What are you going to wear to the press conference?"

"My navy suit, blue shirt that looks good on TV, and probably a navy tie. How about you?"

She put up her delicate hands. "I'm strictly behind the scenes. No appearances for me."

"Come on. You're gorgeous. You'd make great TV."

"I'm shy," Bella said with a sly smile.

Mark burst out laughing. His eyes crinkled in that quirky way. "Shy is the last word that applies to you, but I accept your decision." He returned to his genial mood. "What time is it scheduled?"

"Four o'clock. Time enough to make the evening

11

news and early enough to give downtown workers a reason to leave early. I'm sure there'll be a crowd."

"I take it you have my prepared remarks." He sat back in his chair.

Bella placed another USB on his desk. "There are some preliminary motions to be filed as well."

"Who are you?"

She had his attention. "Does it matter if you win the case?" She smiled and looked up at him from under her long lashes.

"No, as long as you're not acting on behalf of organized crime or dicey campaign financers."

She knew he was only partly joking. "Rest assured, I've no ties to either of those slippery lots."

"Well, at least tell me what I should call you."

"Bella." She stood to leave. As she swiveled her fine ass toward the door, she looked over her shoulder and smiled. "I'll be sure to watch you on the news. Later, Mark."

***

He was impressive. Clearly, they had caught the attorney general's office off-guard as well as the press. Mark made his remarks and then handled questions in an intelligent, affable, and authoritative way. He could be extremely charming and was well aware of his good looks and effect on people. He'd be great in front of a jury.

Bella didn't plan to let this go to a jury. No time for that. Merely the time allowed for her opponent to respond to motions, never mind prepare for a trial, could drag the case on for three or even four years. She wanted to have overwhelming evidence of deliberate and wanton civil rights violations at Commonwealth Psych so even the toughest judge would have to rule for Summary Judgment—a verdict based only on a stack of paper the attorney general couldn't dispute. No need to go to trial. It was rare to win such a verdict, but she wasn't the best legal mind in New York because she played it safe.

One thing in her favor was that the federal court in Richmond was known throughout the United States for its Rocket Docket. Cases were tried faster than in any other court in the country. She planned to use that to her advantage. She wanted Daniel to be well, the hospital closed, and the Coopers to have a fat check before the year was out.

CHAPTER FOUR

Mark look well-rested when he entered his office Monday morning. He'd spent the weekend sailing on the Chesapeake Bay, eating fresh seafood, and sleeping on his thirty-two-foot cutter rigged monohull unimaginatively named *Aquarius*. Alone. There had been plenty of women flirting with him at the bar where he went for sunset drinks, restaurants for dinner, and marina near his boat slip. He was polite and friendly, but he declined even the most obvious invitations.

His blue eyes against a deeply tanned face made him a handsome and delectable man. His face registered surprise when he unlocked the door to his office to find her waiting for him in her usual white leather chair. He almost dropped his latte from the corner café, but recovered quickly. Agile. He pretended to take her presence in stride.

"Good morning. Would you like some of my latte?" he said as he sat behind his desk and turned on his computer.

"No thanks." She was equally nonchalant. "Did

you have a good weekend? Relaxing?"

He checked email and sipped his latte. "Very nice."

"Good. There's a lot to be done. We're going for Summary Judgment."

He lost his cool demeanor. "No one gets one from this district. No one." He was polite but adamant.

"Actually, there was one in 1977 and another in 1992."

"Great, then. Not in the past twenty-five years." He stopped pretending to pay attention to anything or anyone other than her.

"Does that matter?" she asked as she crossed and re-crossed her long legs.

"Of course. These judges are old boys. I'm not really an old boy, and you certainly aren't."

"Are you suggesting there is corruption or collusion within the federal judiciary? Surely, those judges would be reported to the ethics committee or persuaded to recuse themselves." She looked at him with those blue eyes wide in innocence. Sugared sarcasm.

He stood, walked around his glass desk, and leaned against it in front of her. "You obviously don't know a thing about politics in Virginia. These old boys have a life of privilege, educations at St. Matthew's or Choate followed by college at the University of Virginia or Washington and Lee, and employment at their families' business, or if they're really rich, none at all. Their free time is spent drinking, playing golf, and going to appropriate charitable functions. They marry girls from College of Charleston or the now defunct Sweetbriar and raise two proper children. Outsiders are not only viewed with suspicion but are unwelcome. Everyone has a reason to keep—collusion, as you call it—secret. No one breaks the code."

He reached behind him to get his cup from his desk and downed the rest of his latte.

"Doesn't that describe you?" Bella asked sweetly.

"Technically," he admitted. Bella hadn't chosen Mark to be the perfect partner in her scheme to bring down Commonwealth Psych by accident. Her research was meticulous. She knew exactly who he was and what his standing was within Richmond society. He'd gone to St. Matthew's, University of Virginia, and UVA Law School. His father was a partner at the most prestigious firm in Richmond, which meant the state. His mother was a former debutante turned alcoholic from sheer boredom. He had a sister who'd fled to Australia after high school.

"Without the debutante and the two children," Bella added.

"Yes," he snapped. She made a mental note of his sore spot.

"I don't see a problem. If you're one of them, they'll surely listen to any effort to protect them from the rumor mill or even the whisper of an ethics committee investigation."

He didn't respond.

"If you're going to win this case, and my intention is to make sure we do, you'll have to up your political game. I don't care if you choke doing

16

it."

"Who are you again? Some ruthless New York…"

"Excuse me, Mr. Hoffman, but I've transcribed office voice mails from the weekend." A prim twenty-something in a Tory Burch dress walked in spreading a faint scent of Jo Malone's Orange Blossom fragrance and placed the paper on his desk. She left without speaking to Bella.

"Damn it, I told her to email me the transcriptions." Mark's attention was temporarily diverted from Bella.

"Replace her," Bella suggested with a shrug.

"You're going to tell me how to run my office, too?" Mark raised his voice.

"You need a smart, computer-savvy bitch guarding your practice, not some debutante who hasn't managed to land one of those husbands you were describing." He would inevitably admit she was right. "Perhaps I was mistaken. I thought you worked by yourself in order to do things less traditionally." She smiled. "May we please return to the discussion of strategy?"

He walked to his frosted glass door and closed it. He sat in the twin of Bella's white leather chair and faced her.

"Bella, you can't order me around. This is my firm. I have one associate. We're not really associates; we share office space. I like it that way. I choose my clients. I choose my battles."

She stood. "I underestimated you. I thought you were a winner. A man who would do anything to win this case. Not only for the Coopers, but for the despicable way the Psycho Killer—who apparently doesn't have a name, according to the media—was left untreated and unattended in that fourteenth century dungeon. People in this state are entitled to mental health care, and they're not getting it. Their civil rights aren't even a consideration. If you want to maintain the status quo, win a small sum for the Coopers, and let the old boys continue to run things as their personal fiefdom, fine. Your father will be proud. I'm not interested."

He called as she walked toward the door.

"Stay. We'll work it out."

Men were so easy.

CHAPTER FIVE

She only had to make three phone calls before she found who she wanted. Dressed in a black cashmere tank dress with tiny sequins to make it sparkle when she walked, Bella made her way to Toxic, one of the area's three dance clubs, Thursday night at midnight. Opal was at the door determining who was allowed to enter, whether they were near the legal age for admission, and checking out the guys who wanted in. One side of Opal's black hair was shaved. The other side hung in a steep triangle to touch her shoulder. She had colorful tattooed bracelets on her right wrist and a string of gemstones in her left ear. She was spilling out of the top of her red tube dress.

She looked amused when Bella approached. Bella wasn't quite old enough to be a patron's mother, but she was too old for this club.

"ID," Opal said in a bored tone.

"Oh, no, Opal. I'm here to see you. Could we talk at your next break?"

Without demonstrating any surprise or interest,

Opal checked the time on her phone. "I'll take it now." She texted someone, and a stoned guy in his early twenties slunk over to replace her.

"Take as long as you'd like," he said.

"Right," Opal said to no one in particular as she left her post and walked outside.

"Is there somewhere we can go to talk?" Bella asked.

"Here's good. Down at the end of the building. I can smoke there." She pulled out a tin of hand-rolled cigarettes, lit one, and inhaled. Tobacco, not dope. Deep, rich aroma. Higher quality than anything the cigarette manufacturers offered.

"What do you want?" Opal inhaled the first drag of her cigarette.

Bella liked that Opal got right to the point. "I'm here to offer you a job."

"Why would I want one?" She continued to enjoy her smoke.

"It involves accessing computer files that aren't necessarily available to the public." Bella gave her a just-us-girls look.

"No way. I'm not screwing with people's credit cards and money." Opal flicked ash onto the gravel.

"I'm a lawyer. It's for a case my colleague and I are working on against the state for treating patients at Commonwealth Psychiatric as less than human. It allows people like Evan Cooper to be killed when he was just there to kick smack. It's a legit case in federal court. The information is available through the Freedom of Information Act, but processing requests stalls cases for years. Especially in a case against the state. We need to speed it up."

"Okay. Why me?"

"Do you have to ask? I made three phone calls and got your name. You're an underground celebrity."

"When would I do this?"

"That's the catch. You also have to be the receptionist and work from ten to six Monday through Friday."

"Oh, man. A straight job." She flicked her ash disgustedly.

"In a law firm."

"Do I look like I want to work in a law firm?"

"You look like you want to do anything you find interesting," Bella replied in her seductive voice.

"What would I have to wear?" Opal's tone suggested mild interest.

Bella made that wonderful song-like laugh. "No flip-flops, not too much cleavage, and no navel. You don't ask what you'd be paid, but you want to know what to wear?"

"Some things are deal-breakers." Back to smoking.

This girl was smart. She liked her.

"What's the pay?"

"Just over ten grand a month and a six-figure bonus if we meet the deadline we've set."

"High or low six figures?"

"Low. You're the best but not the only name I have."

"When would I start?" She put out the cigarette and crushed it with the heel of her platform sandal.

"Monday. At ten o'clock."

"You're legit?"

Bella handed her Mark's business card. "Legit."

"Okay. Sure."

Bella offered her hand to Opal, who apparently had never shaken hands before. She awkwardly took Bella's hand and touched her palm. Nicely. Not too hard. Not squishy.

"What's your name?" Opal called as Bella walked away.

"Bella."

CHAPTER SIX

Bella strolled into the office about eleven Friday morning and went straight to Mark's office.

"You were right," he said. He was pacing. "Damn it."

"Good morning, Mark." She sat on the white leather sofa facing the sun. "I usually am."

"What?" he asked.

"Right. About what specifically?" She crossed her legs.

He held out his hand and showed her a small pile of black, electronic bits. "Tom's office was bugged. Whoever did it didn't realize I have the smaller office because it offers more daylight. Tom's is larger, so they assumed it was mine. The restroom and the library/conference room were bugged too."

"Well, I hope Tom hasn't been indiscreet," she said.

"That's not the point. The AG's office isn't taking this well. They're..."

"Ruthless. Like me." She smiled.

"How could they have done it? I have an alarm

system. They couldn't just waltz in here during the day."

Bella smoothed her skirt. "Mark, you're a very bright man, but your thinking is completely inside the box. I know exactly how it was done, by whom, and that she should be fired immediately. Her replacement will be starting Monday at ten o'clock." She shrugged. "More or less."

When Mark realized Bella meant the debutante, he was adamant she wouldn't have done it. "Her? No way."

"Mark, let's not waste time. Someone probably offered her a date with a blond Kappa Alpha two years out of UVA. She thinks she'll be engaged in six months."

Bella watched Mark's face change as realization struck him that the old boys were playing dirty with him too. He wasn't in the inner sanctum.

"Pay her for two weeks and tell her she's no longer needed. No accusations. Just *fini*. Tell her now. I always hate it when HR fire people at the end of a Friday afternoon."

He sighed and started toward the door.

"Mark," she called, "Don't offer anything more—like a good reference—for her tears." Men were oblivious. "Unless, of course, you want to perpetuate the old boy approach."

He gave her a look of incredulity. Then he caught her train of thought. One shed tear and he'd have offered a good reference, an extra week of pay, and a vacation.

Within five minutes, the debutante was gone. By noon, a new security system, including surveillance monitors, had been ordered. Soundproofing for Mark's office had been ordered earlier in the week. By Monday morning, the office would be secure.

***

"I need to get out of here. Do you want to go for a drive?" Mark said after finalizing the order for the new security system.

"Certainly." It had been a rough morning for a soft guy like him. How ridiculous for him to trust a debutante just because she had a pedigree.

"Let's go. I need fresh air," he said.

Bella was happy to let him take charge, so she didn't ask any questions and let him do what he needed.

They walked through the rear door of the office and into the garage. He put on aviator sunglasses and opened the passenger door to an older model silver Jaguar XK convertible. She slid in. He got in, started the car, and roared out of the garage. No music. Top down. He maneuvered skillfully to get out of Richmond and onto some less travelled roads. Once there, he opened up the car to fifth gear and they flew down straight roads, around wide curves, and up into hilly country. After about an hour, he slowed to the speed limit.

Exhilarating. Bella loved every second of it. No fear. Just pure joy at the feeling of flying. Being a ghost had its perks. Mark pulled over in a sandy patch near a sign that read Polo Grounds. He opened a bottle of water and offered it to her. "No thanks," she said, and he slugged it back.

"Man, I needed that."

Of course he did. It certainly beat sailing for releasing tension. She hated sailing what with all the getting up and down and knotting and unknotting ropes and watching the boom. A sleek, powerful cigarette boat was fine with her. Turns out cars could be equally thrilling.

He turned in his seat to look at her. "You look like the Cheshire cat. Your smile is a mile wide."

"That was fun." She pushed a strand of hair back under the silk scarf she'd tied over her hair so it wouldn't blow in her face. "What's next?"

He looked like he was going to kiss her but stopped himself. "Not much. Hilly roads the rest of the way."

He got back on the road and drove along green pastures and grassy hillsides until he turned off into a thicket of trees. A hidden lane. No one would know it was there. He drove up what felt like a mile-long drive and then a large, brick, federal-style house came into view. He pulled around back and stopped.

The air was fresh with the smell of grass and hay on this warm afternoon. There was an energy about being around working horse stables. She loved it.

He got out of the car and shouted, "Carlton." A tall, slim man about sixty years old came from a white barn. Mark met him halfway. The two shook hands. Carlton clapped him on the shoulder.

"Didn't know you were coming. Would have gotten some provisions."

"I didn't know I was coming. I just had to get out of town. Somehow found myself here."

26

"Is that right? Did you tell that pretty lady where you were headed?"

Mark laughed and shook his head. "No, and she didn't ask. It's been a long week."

Bella got out of the car and leaned against it in her ivory silk suit. She waited three beats, took off her heels, and walked barefoot in the soft springy grass to meet the two men.

"Bella, this is Carlton, my uncle and head of the farm. Knows everything there is to know about horses. It's people he doesn't like."

Bella gave him one of her most dazzling smiles. "Carlton, I'm pleased to meet you." She shook his hand and let her finger tips linger just slightly too long. "I understand your sentiments well."

"Do you ride?" Carlton asked.

"Not in several years." Not since the house in Connecticut and her and her husband's grey and two mahogany bays. A true lifetime ago. No, she wouldn't remember life with her husband. Ever. She'd couldn't relive his death and the pain that followed.

"Go on in the house," Carlton said. "Fix yourself drinks. I'll be up in a while."

Mark took her hand and led her through the back portico, onto a wide brick veranda, and into the dining room. "What are you drinking?"

"Nothing for me, thanks. I'm going to freshen up in the powder room." He nodded toward the right. "Second door."

She closed the door and leaned against it. A handsome, sexy guy who had guts. He just needed some prodding. Carlton must be a Sensitive. She hadn't prepared herself to be visible to anyone other than Mark. The horses would notice her, but they would instinctively know she was benign to creatures. She repaired her makeup, released her hair from the scarf, and shook it until it fell in loose waves around her shoulders. She took off her suit jacket under which she wore a sleeveless silk blouse. She'd do. For now.

CHAPTER SEVEN

He waited in the kitchen. "Do you want to walk? Stretch your legs?"

"Yes, I would." She'd enjoy it, and Mark needed to clear his head further. Mark took her hand and led her outside. This time, he led her away from the barn toward the pastures. She saw two mares grazing in the distance. A stallion was posed magnificently under a tree two pastures away.

They stopped at a nearby pasture and rested their arms on the weathered wood fence. Bella looked straight ahead and whistled softly. She didn't want to startle the stallion. "Who is that bad boy?"

Mark laughed. "God. Or so he thinks. He was bred here. He's Carlton's baby. Big, secret plans." He spread his arms wide.

"He's majestic, certainly." She knew horses, and this one was exceptional. "What's his barn name?" she asked.

"Macho," Mark said as he rolled his eyes.

Bella laughed. "It fits." Carlton knew what he was doing. He was smart and didn't mind getting his

29

hands dirty. The complete opposite of Mark's father, who was bright enough but didn't like heavy lifting, according to her sources.

They walked for about a mile in silence until Mark realized she was barefoot. He'd changed into someone's old shoes and hadn't thought about her. "I'm sorry. I didn't think about shoes for you. I'm sure there are plenty of women's shoes here. I'm an idiot."

She leaned into him. "No, just a man getting out of his head for an afternoon. I don't mind. I can recognize poison ivy. I doubt there are any other dangers."

The sun was low in the sky. Mark took her hands and faced her. "Would you mind if it weren't just for the afternoon? We could spend the night, laze around tomorrow or go into Middleburg, and drive back in the afternoon."

She didn't say anything. She always thought it best to let the man come to her.

"Bella, I didn't plan this. I didn't plan to bring you here overnight. I need to clear my head. I knew the old boys were corrupt and there was very little they wouldn't do, but I didn't think they'd do it to me."

She let him think about what he'd said. He'd been cut from the herd.

"Why do you think they bugged Tom's office and not yours? Surely, the debutante could point them in the right direction."

"That bothered me too, but she probably was told just to let people in when Tom and I were both out. They wouldn't tell her what they were doing.

She's a woman. She didn't need to know details."

"Hmmm." Bella sighed. He was probably right.

"Do you mind staying overnight?" He stopped abruptly. "You must think I'm truly an idiot. Of course, you have plans. You agreed to a drive, not an overnight. If we leave now, it won't be too late when we get back."

She kissed him lightly. A feathery touch on his lips. "No plans. I'm happy to stay."

He seemed relieved. He really did need some time to adjust his thinking. Those old boys weren't just political manipulators. They were dangerous when thwarted. It was startling to him. Spending some time with his uncle who'd rejected that life wouldn't hurt. Carlton knew what it was to be an outsider and didn't seem to mind.

When they started back toward the house, Mark told her about Carlton. His father's younger brother. Married until his wife ran off with one of the owners of the horses he trained and boarded. Not good for a trainer's reputation. She left the kids— two boys and a girl—with Carlton. The brick house was unimaginatively named Redstone and had been in the family for generations. Mark's dad, Carlton, and another uncle had spent their summers here as children, but Carlton was the only one who'd stayed. The rest of the family visited on occasion. Very low key. No fraternal rancor about ownership.

Carlton was grilling fish when they returned.

"Smells divine. Dill, is it?" Bella asked.

Carlton looked surprised. "Yes. Doesn't usually go with fish, but I like it. You two are staying for dinner and overnight, aren't you?"

31

"Yes, if you don't mind," Mark said.

"Yes to the second for me," Bella said. "I had a breakfast meeting this morning that was too much. What I'd like now is a bath and a soft bed. My feet are filthy. Do you have some socks I could wear so I don't track dirt through your home?"

She looked at Carlton. She didn't flutter her eyelashes. That would be too much, but she'd still managed to charm him.

"No, go right on up. Here," he handed Mark the grill tongs, "I'll show you your room."

He grabbed what was essentially her briefcase full of human accoutrements. She took an apple and a glass of water for show and silently followed him through a long hallway, up a classic wood staircase, and to the back of the second floor. He opened a door into a lavender room overlooking a pasture to the east.

"This is my daughter's room. She's on the show circuit now. She's taller than you, but she must have something that will fit you. Night clothes and such."

"It's lovely, Carlton. I'll be comfortable here and able to see the sun rise. Thank you."

He hesitated. "It's nice that he brought someone here. It's been too long."

Bella lightly touched Carlton's arm. "My father always used to say there's no time schedule for overcoming loss. Sometimes, it never happens." She didn't know what Mark's loss was and didn't ask. Bella needed his head in the game. If Mark needed an overnight or two in the country, fine with her.

Carlton nodded. "Good night, Bella. Holler if

you need anything."

She smiled and shut the door. Being visible for a full day was a lot. She needed a break.

CHAPTER EIGHT

Bella needed to see Daniel. She loved him and wanted to at least see, if not talk, to him. She also wanted to make sure his recovery was progressing. She and Mark had returned late Saturday afternoon. He seemed more relaxed and focused after a getaway from Richmond and its old boys and politics. She loved the feeling of flying in the roadster on the way back more than on the trip to Redstone. How she wished she could fly. Being a ghost should have perks beyond being invisible.

Daniel lived with his mother Selma in an attached villa in a pastoral gated retirement community with jogging paths, a swimming pool, and a fitness center. Although he was probably the youngest resident, Daniel needed someone to supervise his schedule of medication and meals. Living with his mother made sense. After two stints in Commonwealth Psych, he was probably happy to be anywhere that was pleasant and comfortable with a kind person for company. He also had a dog and cat. Bella suspected he had a special affinity for the dog.

Bella had inspected Selma's villa while Daniel and Selma were out, so she knew the layout. Tonight, she had to remain invisible to everyone, including Daniel. That took concentration, but the house was too small and open to hide. It was a single-story house with a master bedroom at one end, two small bedrooms at the other, and a family room/kitchen between them.

Bella had followed Daniel's affairs while he was at Petersburg. Selma and Daniel's brother Rob had despaired of him ever being well enough to be released from the hospital to return home. The house he'd shared with his wife and daughter was empty. Daniel's daughter boarded at St. Margaret's in Richmond and spent summers at camp or in Charleston with her maternal grandparents. Should Daniel ever be released, the house was too large for one man and a girl who would rarely visit. In the meantime, maintenance was expensive. Rob had held an estate sale for the furnishings and sold the house, although he'd probably stored a box of keepsakes for Daniel. Rob always chided Daniel about being a packrat, but he was kind enough to know his brother might want something from his previous life, especially photographs, should he ever be released from Commonwealth Psych.

Selma's villa was new and modern and decorated in tones of blue, white, and an occasional splash of yellow. Both bedrooms had identical furniture—a maple single bed, dresser, and yellow chair. Selma had obviously let the girl decorate her room, but the only personal touches seemed to be a quilt probably made by her mother and a scraggly stuffed rabbit on the bed. The poignant touches were photographs of the girl with Holly and Ivan; the girl, her mother, Daniel, and the family dog Abbie; and the girl with her mother the Christmas before Bella killed her mother. The girl's maternal grandmother had been excised from the photograph. A rolling acrylic desk was tucked neatly in a corner.

Daniel's room could have been in a mental health center. The furniture was a duplicate of the girl's room. Nothing personal. Nothing. The top of the bureau was empty. The bed had built-in end tables and lights. Nothing was on either of the tables. No book, no phone charger, not even a box of tissues. Bella wondered if Daniel was allowed to have a phone. There was an extra coverlet folded at the end of the bed. Daniel must still get chilled with panic and need extra warmth. Bella hated Daniel living in a place so devoid of any sentiment.

Bella double checked her cloak of invisibility before taking up her post just inside the front door. Daniel might sense her if she wasn't careful. She was surprised to find the girl visiting the first weekend of the school year and that they were home on a Saturday night. Daniel and the girl were in the family room. Selma was in her master bedroom.

Poor Selma. Eighty years old and still responsible for her adult son. Bella had read the custody agreement in its entirety. Rob and the maternal grandparents shared custody, but someone had to be with Daniel and the girl at all times.

Subsequent filings showed the mother-in-law to

be a harpy determined to ruin what was left of Daniel's life, even going so far as to try to block the sale of the house Daniel owned because she felt half of the proceeds should go to her as Daniel's late wife's mother. Whatever lawyer had filed such a frivolous motion should've been sanctioned. Houses are indivisible in the case of one spouse predeceasing the other.

Daniel rarely saw the girl. Rob had fought and won at least one week of vacation in the summer and one or two days during a to-be-determined holiday. Tonight, Selma must have decided Daniel and the girl called Kate could watch a soccer game on TV one room away from her without incident.

At the first commercial, Kate muted the remote.

"Dad, what does depression feel like?" She wore jeans and a tee shirt with a beaded choker and sat curled on the sofa. Daniel was at the other end of the sofa sitting erect with his feet on the floor. He was thin, but appeared to be slightly more muscular. The white hair still startled Bella. His eyes were blank. He hadn't been watching TV. He'd been staring blindly in that direction.

The girl caught his attention and he became alert.

"What kind of depression, Kate?" he asked and turned to look at her.

She gave him the exasperated look only a sixteen-year-old girl can give a parent. "I didn't know there were different kinds. I want to know what it feels like inside. I've read about it on the internet, but I can't find any stories by people who have it. Do you just feel really sad?"

He released a long sigh. Bella ached for him.

37

He'd had years now of people asking him how, when, and for how long he'd felt Mørk. He must be tired of answering questions and answered by rote, but the person asking now was his daughter. He'd be honest with her.

He looked at the floor. "Everyone's different, Kate. For me, a basic episode makes me feel down. Everything loses its color. Not a lot. Just faded. I feel like the rest of the world is going at a faster speed than I am. Everything people do seems exaggerated. Like they're laughing too loud or talking too fast or making fools of themselves. I don't feel out of it. More like under it. I wake up to rain and feel relieved when the weather matches my mood. People expect less of me on rainy days."

"How do you know it's just not a bad day?"

"It feels that way every day for at least two weeks. Like a slump. Then it either gradually gets better or gets a lot worse."

Ivan trotted in from the kitchen to sit on Daniel's feet. This must be painful for Daniel to discuss. He probably had no clue why she was asking. Bella realized the girl was starting to feel it herself.

"Mom said you named your episodes."

Daniel flinched at the word mom. "I did. I thought if I could name it, I could control it or at least manage it. I named it Mørk—a shortened version of the Norwegian *Mørketid,* or Dark Night."

"Why? We're not Norwegian."

This would be interesting. Daniel shifted in his seat. Of course, he'd told this story repeatedly to doctors, therapists, and groups, but telling the girl would feel different. Maybe.

"Bella, the woman who broke my heart, named it in college. I remember feeling really sad twice for about two weeks—always in late fall, but she pulled me out of it. She'd studied Nordic literature and there were a lot of references to the endless nights at the Arctic Circle during winter. It was the time of dark nights. Some people chose to call it blue nights or blue time because of the Aurora Borealis colors. Either way, it fit what I felt."

The girl stroked the grey and white cat Holly as if pondering the next question.

"How do you feel in the worst?"

"Kate, do you really want to talk about this?" He looked pained.

She sat straight and raised her voice. "Yes, I do. No one told me anything truthful for a long time. Now you're here, and I can ask you directly. I want you to tell me the truth."

The girl wasn't stupid and she wasn't going to let Daniel get away with anything.

"Look at me, Dad."

Daniel turned toward her and sat quietly. His arm rested on the arm of the sofa. He spoke so softly Bella could hardly hear him from her post by the front door.

"The very worst was when I didn't follow." He stopped. Apparently, he couldn't say Bella's name easily. "I didn't follow my girlfriend to Paris after college. I stubbornly refused to go with her to where she said I'd find great resume-building opportunities. I insisted on going to business school in Miami. It was awful. Miami Beach wasn't like it is now. No clean beach. Just drug dealers, nursing

39

homes, and vacant buildings. I didn't like school. I didn't speak Spanish and felt at a real disadvantage. I hated it."

"Did you speak French?"

"What? No." He looked confused.

"Why would you have been better in Paris if you didn't speak French?" She sounded puzzled.

"Sweetheart, I'd have been with her. She made everything wonderful and exciting. She was fluent in French and would insist I learn something. Italian. Spanish. Russian. Anything so I'd be bilingual if I was going to have an international business."

The girl sighed. She'd probably tired of hearing about Bella. Maybe not. Maybe this was the first she was hearing about Bella from Daniel.

"So, you were sad and lonely in Miami. Then what happened?"

Yes, Bella wanted to know that too.

"She kept writing me, urging me to come to Paris, to quit school, or even come for a visit. I didn't want to admit I was wrong. She finally sent me a letter that said she'd been offered several opportunities after the Sorbonne and if I wasn't planning to come, then she'd have to move on without me. I thought she'd met someone else."

"Why would you think that?"

"Because depression clouded my thinking and deep down I didn't believe I deserved her."

"Why not?" The girl frowned.

"I couldn't believe someone like her could love me. I just couldn't."

"That's pretty pathetic. What did you do?"

Daniel paused a moment. Even his sixteen-year-old daughter knew his reasons for not following Bella were lame. "I just sort of stopped living. I didn't go to class or meals or the library. I stopped leaving my room in the graduate student dorm. I cried all the time. I tried to commit suicide by taking a bottle of ibuprofen."

"Dad." The girl jumped to her feet. "You tried to kill yourself? You never told me. Does everyone else know but me?"

Daniel flinched at her sudden movement to stand in front of him. Hands on hips. Outrage on her face.

He spoke softly. "Yes, I tried to kill myself. That memory is buried deep. Gran, Suzanne, and Rob know, but no one else. I never told your mother."

"You lied to her?" She was waffling between being angry and incredulous. She turned away from Daniel.

He didn't call out and continued to speak quietly. "I didn't lie. I told her about Mørk. She didn't ask for details other than what it meant to us as a couple. I didn't think she'd care about a suicide attempt in grad school."

The girl sat. She didn't say anything as though she was processing this news. She decided to continue what was a startling conversation with her father. "You tried to kill yourself and then what?"

"Someone, maybe the resident assistant, called 911. I woke up in a hospital. My dad was there. He drove me in my car back to Richmond when I was released. I don't remember officially withdrawing from school. I just went home and lived in my childhood bedroom for almost three years."

41

The girl looked stunned. "That's a long time. What did you do there?"

Bella empathized with the teenaged girl. Young adults usually couldn't wait to be rid of their parents after college.

"Mostly slept at first. I was so tired. A lot of it was grief. I'd lost her, and I felt like my life was over. I just couldn't see myself ever leaving my bedroom. My parents had a friend of a friend who was a psychiatrist who agreed to visit me at home. He didn't think I needed to be hospitalized. He didn't think I had energy enough to hurt my parents or myself. He was right.

"He prescribed medication, and the first one didn't work. I couldn't find the strength to stand up. I felt like the distance from my bed to the door was about the length of a football field. It really looked that far to me. I didn't believe anyone who told me it wasn't.

"The second medication sort of worked because I stopped crying, but I couldn't get out of bed or leave my room. Mom brought me meals on a tray. I didn't go downstairs for probably six months. I didn't want to do anything other than lie in my room with my dog."

Kate didn't answer immediately. Bella imagined it must seem unbelievable that her father couldn't leave his bedroom to go downstairs to eat dinner with her grandparents. From what Daniel had told her, the girl enjoyed Daniel's parents and was devastated when his father died.

"I'm sorry, Dad."

Daniel looked at her kindly. "Sweetheart, it was

a long time ago."

"How did you get better?"

"The psychiatrist tried different medications and one finally worked. Slowly, I moved back into life. I felt better. I had physical therapy because I'd spent so much time in bed that my muscles had atrophied. Once I was able to walk around, the psychiatrist insisted I leave my room and my parents' house and go to his office for visits. He required me to take daily walks around the cul de sac and keep a journal. I hated that. I think I wrote the word blank every day for a couple of months. That's how I felt. Blank.

"I didn't have any interests. I couldn't concentrate well enough to read even comics in the newspaper. I'd fall asleep watching a movie on TV. Sitcoms were about families or co-workers and I couldn't relate to them."

"But you got better," she prompted.

"After the medication got to full force. I wanted to go outside and move around. I read about sports in the newspaper. I could watch at least half of a football game on a Sunday afternoon with Dad and Rob. One little thing at a time, I got back to being a normal person, but it took about three years. Once I felt semi-normal, I realized I couldn't live with my parents forever. It was a burden for them, and I had to be independent. I had to get a job.

"Kate, I need a break. I'm going to get a Dr. Brown's cream soda. Your favorite. Do you want anything?"

"No," she shook her head, "Not right now." She hugged Holly close and sat very still.

CHAPTER NINE

Bella relaxed while Daniel was in the kitchen. She didn't realize how tense she'd become both from concentrating to keep Daniel from sensing her presence in any way and being so fascinated by his story. She'd picked a great night to check on him. Eavesdropping on whatever he was willing to tell the girl was almost as good as a direct conversation.

Daniel returned to the same spot on the sofa and sipped his soda. He turned the TV off.

The girl dogged him immediately with questions.

"How did you get a job? You didn't have any experience or references."

The corners of Daniel's mouth turned up. "I'd recovered from a long traumatic episode of depression not stupidity. I was a UVA graduate with a degree in economics. I'd taken time off after graduation for medical reasons. That's all any potential employer needed to know.

"I took a civil service job doing something that wasn't hard for me—data entry—that allowed me to adjust to working five days a week. As I got better,

I took jobs that were more interesting, but I never took one that required me to travel or work overtime. I could only work from eight to four and go home. Learning to interact with co-workers scared me. I was nervous they would sense something was wrong with me and tried to avoid them, but eventually, I adjusted. I forced myself to say hello to everyone every day. That was an enormous effort for me."

"Saying hello was a big deal? You're so friendly. I can't imagine that."

"Don't try, sweetheart. Socializing is a skill. I just needed practice. The final piece was when I moved out of my parents' house and into an apartment close to work. I'd never lived independently. I was lost at first, but I made a routine that I followed strictly until I got the hang of it."

"Like what?"

This girl was relentless. She wasn't cutting Daniel even a little slack. She'd probably been in the dark about his emotional life for a long time and was now seizing the opportunity to find the missing pieces about her family history.

"A daily schedule of everything to do that day plus a weekly schedule of doing laundry, grocery shopping, and paying bills. I also had a strict schedule to follow that consisted of taking anti-depressants and seeing my psychiatrist."

"You had that all written down? On a calendar?"

Daniel shook his head. "Three calendars—one for what I had to do every hour, day, and week. I gradually didn't have to look at it every single day.

Back then, no one had cell phones, so I relied on alarm clocks to remind me to do things. I became friendly with neighbors in the apartment complex. I started running. Week by week, I was able to work and maintain my health, an apartment, and a car."

"Didn't you date?"

"Not for a long time. I think I was about thirty. I'd go out with a girl once and that would be it. I compared all of them to Bella and no one ever measured up. I was slow to realize that Bella wouldn't look twice at me. I wasn't anything like the guy she'd known and loved. I was maybe forty percent of who I used to be. I didn't deserve Bella. So, I accepted who I'd become and started dating people who might be interested in who I was then. I got the hang of it eventually, and met your mother the year I turned forty."

Interesting. It took him almost twenty years to even begin to function without her. Bella smiled. Invisibly.

Whether she lived with Daniel or not, the girl had some of his mannerisms. Bella could tell she felt insulted by what he'd said about lowering his standards. Kate narrowed her eyes.

"You mean you settled for Mom."

Daniel's head jerked up. He turned to look at her. "I didn't settle for your mother. Your mother accepted who I was. She'd be the first to say she wasn't brilliant, she didn't like to balance a checking account, and she didn't care about traveling the world. She was fun. She liked her job in marketing. She was athletic, liked to do all kinds of things outdoors that I enjoyed, and she loved cycling.

What she wanted most was a happy family. She said she had everything she'd ever wanted when you were born. Neither of us settled."

Bella thought she saw a few tears from the girl. She, however, thought Daniel had just described the most boring life and marriage possible. A woman who let her husband handle all the finances? Didn't travel? Didn't even want to know what was going on beyond her cul de sac? Really, Daniel had told a nice fairy tale to the girl, but her Daniel settled when he accepted that marriage.

Daniel exhaled two long breaths. Ivan had returned to sit on Daniel's feet, and Daniel reached down to rub him behind the ears. He looked at Kate and not the floor when he spoke. "So, that's how it feels."

This time, Kate sighed. Exasperation. "You haven't told me about being in psych hospitals."

"I really don't want to tell you about that."

"Why not?" She moved so quickly on the sofa the cat jumped off her lap and headed to Selma's room. "You're not sparing me anything. Ever since I was ten years old, I've been the girl whose dad killed her mom and got away with it. No one wants to hear that the charges were dropped. It's a better story to say you went crazy and killed Mom.

"Then, you discovered you had a baby with your girlfriend and you shut yourself in your room stalking her online for months. Gran said I couldn't visit because she was sick. That wasn't true. I couldn't visit because you'd become obsessed and would've ignored me if I'd come. Gran didn't want me to know you were locked in your room stalking your other daughter and writing letters to her or your girlfriend. You couldn't tell them apart."

Odd. Daniel couldn't tell them apart? He'd confused LouLou with her? Bella choked.

Daniel was instantly alert. Ivan looked up at Daniel.

"Did you hear that?"

"No, quit stalling." She sat.

"I heard a woman's voice. Like she was choking or coughing."

"It was probably something Gran's listening to in her room."

Daniel stood and started toward the door. "Stay where you are. I'm going to check the alarm."

Bella vanished through the front door and waited outside as she imagined Daniel checking to see if the alarm was on. She hoped he wouldn't open the front door and look around. She saw him peek through the glass panes at the top of the door and walk back to the den with Ivan at his heels.

Damn. She knew it. She knew Daniel would notice her if she wasn't careful. She'd been careful, but hearing that Daniel had been in such a state as to confuse her with that stubborn LouLou was annoying. She'd been caught off guard. She whisked herself back to her post near the door but as close to the wall as she could get and still hear.

Neither of his daughters were particularly perceptive about Daniel's feelings. Now, this girl was intent on forcing Daniel to relive the nightmare of LouLou's trumped-up stalking charges.

"The FBI investigated. You were arrested again and cut a deal. You went back to Petersburg for six months and another psych hospital after that. I didn't see you for almost a year. Did you think I didn't know the reason? Gran, Uncle Rob, and Aunt Suzanne told me as little as they could so I wouldn't be afraid of you or think that you'd never come back. They said you'd come home much sooner this time.

"Don't you get it? I was older this time. I heard stories on the news. People wanted you put away for good. They said you were a menace. Girls at school talked about it. Everyone knew I was the kid with the crazy dad. Sophia, Josie, and Jada were the only ones who stuck up for me."

Daniel looked like he was about to cry. Bella was certain he'd been in so much confusion and pain that he hadn't thought of anyone, including this girl who, unfortunately, was short and looked like Daniel. Looks that made him handsome didn't do much for a girl. She clearly was athletic. Soccer? Field hockey? Gymnastics?

LouLou was pretty enough. Tall, slim, long blonde hair. She was mostly Bella with enough of Daniel to keep her from being a beauty. Daniel was a handsome man, but certain features from him plagued both LouLou and this one. The size and shape of his eyes, for one. The texture of his hair. Bella was losing focus. She didn't care what either child looked like. They weren't important. She forced herself to concentrate.

"At least tell me what it was like being in the psych hospital the first time," the girl said. Negotiating.

Daniel held the can of soda between his hands.

She knew people with mental illness found holding cold things like glasses of ice with water to be soothing. Daniel must be uncomfortable because he didn't look at the girl. He stared into space again.

"Sweetheart, I don't remember most of it. The last thing I remember was the day we got Holly and Ivan from the animal shelter. I gradually woke up, and the doctors told me I'd been in a catatonic state for about two years. I got better. I took meds, did physical therapy, and saw my psychiatrist every week. Something happened at Petersburg that got me transferred to Richmond Memorial Hospital, but I don't know what it was. I got better and came home. I mean, I moved in here with Gran. Our house, the one where we lived with your mom, had been sold. I accepted that I was too sick to ever work again. I had to figure out a new life. Again."

Daniel didn't remember the incident that frightened him into catatonia. Good. He'd have nothing but the deepest feelings of love toward Bella.

"What about the second time? When you stalked your daughter?"

The girl truly was relentless. She was seizing her opportunity. All great for Bella, who could learn everything from Daniel's perspective.

Daniel took a deep breath before speaking.

"At first, I was shocked—the kind of shock when you hear any life-changing news. You know what that feels like, Kate. I'm sorry you do. I couldn't believe Bella and I had a child."

Daniel waved his hands in enthusiasm. Some soda sloshed on his pants. "It was like this blessing

50

I'd been waiting for all my life. I had a child with Bella and even though she was born in Paris, she lived in Richmond. That had to be fate. I was so happy." He noticed the wet spot on his pants and put the can on a coaster on the end table next to him.

"When LouLou told me she wanted nothing to do with me, I couldn't believe it. I didn't understand and I was hurt. After the shock and happiness wore off, I felt depressed. I sank under things, but this time I had an interest. I wanted to know the child I had with Bella. She resembled Bella. I knew she was a DJ, an artist, and a kind person. She was the only one who paid any attention to me at Petersburg. I had to convince her to be part of my life. Surely, she'd see that a baby born in Paris who grew up and moved not only to the United States, but to Richmond, where he father lived, was fate.

"I couldn't believe she would only see me once. She treated me with suspicion. We met at a public place—Ginter Gardens—and walked around until I asked if we could sit somewhere. I wasn't physically strong yet and tired easily. We had drinks in the tea house, but she didn't stay long. She barely listened to anything I said about how much Bella and I loved each other. She glanced at the picture I showed her of Bella and me. Bella was pregnant with her then. Bella glowed. LouLou just wished me health and walked away."

Look where that got her. Bella wondered again how a child of hers could be so dim. Bella had resorted to killing LouLou's adopted father to get LouLou to realize she had a real father. Even then, she stubbornly refused to see Daniel. LouLou broke his heart. Again.

The girl was getting fidgety. Daniel didn't seem to notice.

"Dad, she's an adult. She's over thirty."

"Why does that matter?" Daniel looked perplexed, but he still didn't look at the girl.

"She had a father. That ambassador. I know terrorists killed him, but she didn't need a replacement. Did you really think you were just going to step in and she'd be all happy to have an extra father?"

"Yes, Kate, I did. I realize now it was too much to ask of a woman who not only was an adult and working, but was fragile. I wouldn't have wanted a new father at thirty, although I'm not a normal example."

"Didn't you think about me?" she yelled and stood directly in front of him so he had to look at her.

This should be good. Did he?

"Not when I was obsessed, Kate. I didn't think about anyone except her. I'm sorry."

The girl looked like he'd slapped her and stood frozen in front of Daniel. Poor man. Sweet, loving Daniel who wouldn't intentionally hurt anyone seemed to decimate everyone around him. Bella wasn't sure whether he was forthcoming because he was an honest man or whether he didn't realize how much pain the truth had inflicted. Probably both.

"At least you told me the truth," the girl whispered. "Everyone else lied to me or glossed over the details of the story. I'm sixteen, but I've experienced a lot."

"I know, Kate, I know. I'm sorry. I am." He didn't try to hug her. "I didn't know what the girls at school said about me. That must have been awful."

She was moving around the room, her voice rising. "It still is. You're not getting it. The first thing anyone I meet thinks about is the girl whose dad killed her mother and was at Petersburg for years. The second thing is that I'm the girl whose dad stalked her half-sister and had to go to Petersburg. It's always going to be like that. Even if I move to Ethiopia, the story will eventually get out. It's okay. That's part of who I am, but it's not all. I just want to know enough so I'm not blindsided when some random detail gets thrown at me."

This time he did stand and hug her. She hugged back, but she didn't cry.

She sat on the sofa and fiddled with her bracelets. "Tell me the rest, Dad. About the obsession."

Daniel finished his soda. "After I was removed from contact with anyone except medical people, I got some perspective. In therapy groups, women talked about what it felt like to be stalked. All of their stalkers wanted to hurt or kill them, but the stalking itself scared them just as much. They were on guard every day.

"I got a new anti-depressant and I started to think about other people again. I no longer wanted to lie in my room and think about her all the time. I remembered you, Gran, Rob and Suzanne, and the people at the animal shelter. I remembered Holly and Ivan. Gradually, I got back to normal. My normal, that is. I was already far from the man I was when you, your mom, and I were a family. I was much less than that. Now, normal for me is never feeling I'm in synch with the world. I take anti-depressants continuously now. My illness is considered chronic. Like diabetes. I have to check myself every day to see if I feel like Mørk is coming.

"My normal means I'm not able to work or do lots of things people do without a second thought. I do have feelings. I love you. I look forward to seeing you and hearing about your life. I love Holly and Ivan. I hate that Gran can't relax and enjoy herself. She has to make sure I'm okay when I'm with you. I hate that you have to board at St. Margaret's and visit one weekend per month. I've accepted it, though. I can't fight it. The court is never going to give a man who has had two stays at Petersburg custody of anyone. That's the whole story."

The girl sat quietly. Selma came in looking frail. Cooperating with the FBI investigation into Daniel for stalking LouLou must have been painful. Her home had been searched and her son taken away. The woman looked weary, but her voice was soft and sweet.

"Everything all right in here? Sounds awfully quiet."

Quiet? The girl had been pacing and yelling just a while ago. Of course, after the story was out, both Daniel and the girl sat on opposite ends of the sofa lost in their own thoughts. Poor Selma. She couldn't even sit in her bedroom on a Saturday night and read or watch TV or listen to music without having to check on her adult son and his teenage daughter. She had to referee to prevent either or both from getting hurt.

Daniel looked at his feet and absent-mindedly rubbed Ivan's head. The girl looked up and said, "We're having a talk. About college."

"College?" Selma asked. "You're only in the first semester of your junior year of high school. Are you thinking about college already?"

"Yes. I take the PSAT this spring and visit colleges over the summer to decide what I want. Applications are due in November. The pressure is on."

Selma sat. "I'd no idea. Way back when Rob and Dan were choosing colleges, there really were only two choices. UVA and Virginia Tech. Neither was interested in science so it was UVA. We never doubted they'd be admitted." Selma smiled at Daniel.

Relieved of the burden of conversation with the girl, Daniel sat quietly, staring in the direction of his mother and rubbing Ivan's ears. The conversation about college was probably new to him but he didn't seem interested.

"Now that I think of it, my friends have seemed pre-occupied around March when acceptance letters are sent."

"Emails, Gran."

"Emails, then. They hope their grandkids have gotten into the school of their choice. It seems to be very competitive and stressful. Is that how you feel?"

She rolled her eyes. "Of course. Every girl at St. Margaret's who isn't going to College of Charleston or Mary Baldwin is freaking out. My grades are the best. I have a shot at being salutatorian and I'm taking prep classes for the PSAT, but the schools I want are really competitive."

"What schools are those?" Selma asked in her soft, southern voice.

"My first choice are ones that have a veterinary graduate school. I think if I go there as an undergraduate, I'll have a better shot at admission to the vet school. Those are Cornell, Georgia, and Penn. Two of those are Ivies. They're almost impossible to get into. Then there's Virginia Tech and Florida. If I can't get into any of them, I'm thinking about Hollins. It has one of the best pre-vet programs without a vet school and includes study abroad programs. It's focused on horses because Hollins is known for its national equestrian championships, but I don't want to be a big animal vet. I want to be a companion animal vet."

"Gracious, Kate. You've given this a great deal of thought and you're just sixteen. Don't you want to go somewhere fun? I don't mean Greek life, but something a little more balanced. Somewhere new. Like New England or California. Somewhere that offers opportunities to study abroad, to live in another culture. The world is huge, and all you've experienced is one elite group of girls from a small southern city for twelve years."

At least Selma thought outside the box. Bella wished Mark had a little of Selma's open-mindedness.

Selma continued. "St. Margaret's has been wonderful for you because it's given you continuity during some difficult times. I'm grateful you've been there for your entire education, but I think the school has a myopic view of the world. Your dad and I aren't pushing you away, but I think it would be good for you to relax a little and go to some other region of the country or even out of the country. You're a talented photographer. Wouldn't you like to go somewhere that offers even more advanced photography courses than what you've taken at St. Margaret's and at VCU? You haven't said that's something you want to do professionally, but improving your craft is a creative outlet. The whole world is out there to be photographed. Besides, Hollins is all women. Do you really want to go to another same-sex school? For horses?"

The girl laughed. "Okay, I'll rethink that one." She was quiet for a moment and then said, "Gran, I never thought about seeing the world, living somewhere long enough to experience life outside Richmond, and having a whole new place to photograph. Thanks. You're a smart lady."

Selma smiled and stood. "I was on my way to get more tea. Would anyone like anything?"

"No, thanks," chorused Daniel and the girl.

"Then I'll be on my way."

CHAPTER TEN

The girl hadn't turned the TV back on. She still had more to say.

"Dad, when you had your earliest times with depression, were you under a lot of stress?"

Daniel struggled to resume concentration. He'd seemed relieved that Selma had taken charge of the conversation and had returned to staring at nothing in particular.

"No. Like Gran said, Rob and I grew up in a different time. We went to school, played sports, and dated. I don't remember school ever being hard. I never stressed about anything. My lacrosse coach would yell, but it wasn't personal. I'd get excited when the Redskins played the Giants, but I never really had stress. I felt the same way at UVA. I majored in economics, which came easily to me. Bella was the best girlfriend in the world. I was happy. I never worried about exams. So, no, I wasn't stressed."

Bella liked hearing that. She'd been the best girlfriend. World champion girlfriend.

Daniel turned to look at the girl. The light bulb was turning on. He realized what she was asking.

"Kate, you're under stress. Do you wonder if you're starting to feel depressed? Clinically depressed, not just sad and listening to sad songs?"

Tears fell. She nodded.

Daniel paled. He looked like he was going to vomit. He looked torn too, like part of him wanted to run away and part of him wanted to parent the girl. Parenting won.

Daniel moved to sit next to her. He hugged her tightly and let her cry. When she stopped sniffling, she sat upright.

Daniel looked at her. "Tell me how you feel."

"Cotton-y. Like I have cotton in my head where my brain used to be. It takes me longer to do homework. Sometimes, I have to re-read whole pages in English lit. I don't always pay attention when people talk. Jada says I seem space-y. Sophia and Josie haven't said anything, but Sophia is killing herself to be valedictorian and class president and volunteer of the year so she'll get into Brown. Josie spends time with her boyfriend and talks about him a lot. I definitely tune that out."

"Why? Why don't you care about Josie's boyfriend?" Daniel looked puzzled. Bella was certain he'd never given his daughter's social life any thought.

"She can do so much better. She's beautiful. I think she's flattered that a senior from St. Matthew's likes her. I'm just going to sit on the sidelines until she's done with him."

"St. Matthew's? Aren't they all gay?" Daniel

asked seriously. He seemed to have no filter.

The girl laughed. Bella too.

"No, they're just soft. Privileged. Not smart. Getting by on their last name. I guess the kind of life Gran was talking about."

Like Mark.

"Do you have boyfriend problems?"

Daniel so did not want to have this conversation. He looked extremely uncomfortable. His right knee was bouncing and he reached for Ivan.

"No, Dad. I date, but I'm sixteen. I've got lots of time. The dating pool isn't so great, either. I've known most of these guys since kindergarten. They weren't cool then and they didn't become cool."

Daniel seemed to get that.

"How long have you felt cotton-y?"

The girl shrugged. "About a month."

"Have you ever felt like this before?" he asked tenderly.

She shook her head. "I sometimes get PMS and feel crabby, but not cotton-y all the time."

Poor Daniel. He was going to have a stroke if he pursued this conversation much further. Boyfriends, PMS, and depression all in one evening.

"I think you should see you doctor to see if there's anything physically wrong with you and a psychiatrist who is an adolescent specialist. Your brain hasn't finished growing, so you need someone who doesn't treat adults."

"Do you think I have it? The internet said it's hereditary."

"Kate, I don't know if you have it. A doctor may not know for certain, but there are medications that can treat your symptoms."

"Dad, I don't want to live a lesser life, like you. I don't want to settle. I don't even have anyone who would take care of me. Gran isn't going to live forever.

"I hate Charleston. I hate Grandmother Elizabeth. Grandfather George is fine, but he lets her walk all over him. Aunt Jane is stoned on pills or alcohol all the time. Aunt Emily only cares about her horses." She'd ticked off all of her mother's family in Charleston.

"The only relatives I like are Rob and Suzanne."

If Daniel noticed she'd omitted him as a possible reliable caretaker, he didn't mention it. Daniel seemed resigned to being a visitor in this girl's life.

"Sweetheart, you're getting way too far ahead of yourself. There's no reason to believe you even have depression. If you do, the medications are so much better than when I was diagnosed.

"I think Gran is right about school. I know all you've ever wanted to be is a veterinarian, but you don't need to concentrate on that now. Your brain isn't ready yet. Go to any college you want. Don't miss opportunities like I did.

"When the time comes for vet school, you'll be five years older. You may have more opportunities than you even know about now. Apply where you want then. You can't plan your life and expect it to happen according to plan. Cut yourself some slack."

Very good, Daniel. Good fatherly advice. Bella was ridiculously pleased that he'd gotten something right.

The girl looked at Daniel with something like

fear. "Doesn't your daughter with your girlfriend have mental illness? You said she was fragile."

Daniel closed his eyes. Bella saw him envision both of his children with mental illnesses.

"Yes, LouLou has schizophrenia. It's awful." He saw he might scare the girl so he pulled back. "Kate, LouLou's illness is rare and serious. Depression can be treated."

"How old was she when she was diagnosed?"

The girl was not going to let Daniel off the hook. She was digging for answers.

"Sixteen," Daniel said softly. "She told me when we were in the same psych hospital before she knew I was her father that she heard voices in her head when it started. Voices that told her to do things she didn't want to do. Hurtful things." He stopped and looked at her closely. "Do you hear voices?"

She shook her head vehemently. "No, no way. I just feel cotton-y."

"You should see the doctors. Rob can set it up. He shares custody with your grandparents so he'll probably tell George. We can leave Elizabeth out of it."

"We can?" The girl brightened immediately.

"George has just as much authority as she does. He acts like he lets Elizabeth get away with a lot, but when something is important, he steps up."

The girl looked relieved. Her uncle and grandfather stood up for her. Her haughty maternal grandmother would no doubt insist there was no mental illness in the pristine Carter family genes.

"For the record," whispered Daniel, "your mom didn't like Elizabeth at all. After St. Margaret's, your mom stayed in Richmond and vowed never to live in Charleston again. She was right. Elizabeth is a pretentious, self-centered, manipulative woman. It's not just you who thinks she's awful. Your instincts to keep some things private from her are right. George kept your mother's secrets and he'll keep yours, too."

The girl hugged him.

Bella had to go. It had been a long weekend. She hadn't spoken directly to Daniel in six years, when she made an appearance on the night he arrived at Petersburg—the night she told him she'd killed his wife and framed him to teach him a lesson. He'd hurt her when he'd promised he wouldn't. He'd been blinded by guilt over his father's death and forgotten his promise. She couldn't let him get away with that. She was as shocked as anyone when her admission of what she'd done had frightened him into catatonia and a long stay at Petersburg.

CHAPTER ELEVEN

Bella had prepared a list of things she needed immediately from Opal. Foremost were the names of all patients at Commonwealth Psych for the past ten years, their diagnosis, discharge date, and current location. From that, she'd eliminate the ones who had died after release. That left people who were still patients, former patients, and patients who died while in residence there.

Mark was already in his office when Bella arrived. "I wanted to get here and make sure everything was in order. Sound-proofing. Security. Surveillance. Things look good. I feel better about having conferences about the case."

Bella scanned the room and admired the seamless upgrades.

"Mark, there's one person we haven't discussed. Do you trust Tom absolutely?"

Mark sat behind his desk. "Yes. He's definitely an outsider. He's from New York and went to Columbia and NYU Law. He moved here with his wife, who is a resident at one of the hospitals. I ran a background check on him before taking him on. He likes the freedom of working with me. He interviewed at some firms, but really didn't like the clandestine old boy feel. I trust him. Why?"

"Double checking. Also, you should probably give him your open cases until this is over."

She saw his reflexive response was anger that she was telling him, once again, how to run his practice. He stifled that, thought about what she suggested, and said, "Good idea. At least in the early stages."

"The AG's response to the complaint is due Monday. We need to be ready with an answer and some motions." Bella tried to seem collegial rather than bossy.

"What do you think they'll do?" Mark asked.

"Stall. Raise jurisdiction, move to dismiss, request more time. We should have responses prepared to file immediately."

"How can we do that? We don't know their strategy."

"Mark, I just told you. What else could it be?" She kept her voice light and sweet so as not to antagonize him. If only he could keep up with her.

She watched him think it through. "Jurisdiction, definitely. They want it out of federal court and back in state."

Right. "They'll appeal. That's why we have to have the best brief ever written on jurisdiction."

"And I suppose you have it." He looked at her expectantly.

She smiled and handed him the flash drive. "I had to do something while you and Carlton were out surveying your kingdom on horseback." He made that crinkly eye movement she liked and smiled.

They were interrupted by the door chime. Ten o'clock. Opal. Bella went to greet her.

"Wow, this really is a legal office. Not a stuffy one, though." She put her backpack on the receptionist's chair. "I followed the dress code." She did a turn.

"Yes, you did." Opal wore a black tee shirt, a red suede mini skirt with fringe, and leopard booties. "Come, I'll introduce you to Mark."

She knocked on Mark's door, introduced Opal to Mark, and let Mark take the lead. Mark didn't say a word about her appearance. "Bella tells me you're the best."

"I am. Where do I sit?"

"The reception area. We have very few clients who come to the office. You'll be free to do your computer work. If the phone rings and Tom or I don't pick up, let it go to voice mail. Voice mail stays on over nights and weekends so any messages left have to be transcribed.

"This case is extremely confidential. All of our clients have confidentiality, but this is a case where we know the opposition is going to try to obtain information unethically. Perhaps, illegally. There's a confidentiality agreement for you to sign. Any questions?" Mark asked politely.

"You were kidding about the voice mail transcription, right?" Opal scoffed.

Mark looked blank. "No."

Opal laughed. "Oh, that is so three years ago.

Install a speech recognition system. It will translate speech to writing while the caller is talking. You can program it to be texted or emailed directly to the person the caller is trying to reach."

"Is it secure?" Mark asked.

"A lot more than relying on a human to transcribe something and get it to the right person."

Mark exhaled. "Okay. Arrange that. Anything else?"

"Not yet," she said.

"Welcome aboard," Mark said and shook her hand.

***

By the end of the day, Opal had a new computer, a secure server, and her personal solution to intruders into the system and a way to cover her tracks when she did her sleuthing. She provided the information Bella had requested, divided it into the three groups, and provided contact information for each patient. The list was 210 people of which 32 had died while in custody. Opal would follow up on the cause of death with the coroner's office.

That left 117 still in custody and 61 who had been released. Bella would narrow down the 61 to those who were capable of making depositions. Daniel was one of them. Mark would depose him. She'd depose LouLou. It was a chance to get to know her better. Perhaps she'd raise her opinion of LouLou.

"Where's your office?" Opal asked when Bella was leaving.

"Oh, I don't have one. I come here for meetings with Mark, but I work on the fly. I'm going to be out of town for a few days. I'll see you Friday. Ask Mark for anything you need."

She dashed out of the office.

CHAPTER TWELVE

"What have you got?" Bella stood just inside the doorway. Ghost or not, she didn't want to touch anything in the seedy, foul-smelling room.

"OD."

Bella and the shifty private investigator stood in a squalid room in what used to be a respectable motel near Fremont Street in downtown Las Vegas. A short five miles from the strip. A galaxy of human misery from the glitz.

"How about opening a window?" Bella asked. She was testing the PI even though she'd used him before.

"Cops won't like it. No."

"You didn't call me here for a junkie OD. What've you got?"

"This junkie," he pointed to the thin man with greasy hair who was wearing only greyish-white boxers and lying on the cigarette-stained carpet that might once have been yellow, "funded his habit with blackmail. He kept meticulous records on computer spreadsheets." He nodded at the old PC

69

desktop on the Formica table. "And in notebooks. Color-coded spiral notebooks. Well organized. Colors for the mark's type of business, preference, and state. Probably a few more, but there's no time to look."

Bella quickly scanned the room. The blackmailer was smart. The computer seemed out of place only if anyone thought about it long enough.

"Cops may or may not take the computer. What would a dead junkie have on a computer? I'm leaving it so the evidence is there if they're smart enough to look for it."

"The notebooks, then." That's the best Bella would get.

"Yeah," the PI said, "you're first on my list. Pick three." He unzipped a small neon green gym bag—a giveaway from one of hotels on the strip—to show about a dozen small notebooks.

"This isn't a homicide, right?" It didn't matter. She'd asked out of habit.

"Pure and simple OD. Fresh blood spots from the needle between his toes." The dead guy's rig was lying by his side not far from his right hand.

"What about photographs?" Pictures were always good when it came to evidence.

He held up a USB drive. "Indexed by name."

"Bank statements?"

"Paper and online. This guy was a real businessman. Probably had backup, but it's not available."

"Someone bigger got them."

The middle-aged man in grey sweatpants and a black hoodie shrugged.

"Let me take a look." Bella made a move to reach into the green bag.

"Nope. Pre-selected. What you want is there." He pointed to a neat stack of notebooks—one green, one black, and one yellow next to the computer. "You can look at them. Wearing gloves."

Bella stifled a laugh. As a ghost, she wouldn't leave fingerprints, but she recovered quickly. "I don't have any. You didn't give me any hints."

"Here." He offered her a pair of yellow gardener's gloves.

With the gloves on, she paged through the notebooks. There was plenty of information in the green and yellow ones. The black one was a bonus.

"I'll take these two plus bank statements for the past five years for the same price."

"Three years on the statements. The pics are on the house."

"Done."

The gardener's gloves were still on when they shook hands.

CHAPTER THIRTEEN

Opal wasn't at her desk when Bella arrived at the office Friday. Mark's office door was open. She took a moment just to consider him. His blue shirt sleeves were rolled up to show tanned muscular arms and hands, he'd loosened his tie so there was a small V at his throat, and his hair was slightly ruffled where he'd run his fingers through it. He looked up and saw her.

He got up from his desk, pulled her inside, and closed the door.

"Glad you're back. I missed you," he said.

She gave him one of her seductive smiles. One of the bonus benefits of the trip was to make him realize he needed her. "Nice to hear," she said.

He sat back behind his desk. "I managed only because of Opal. Where did you find her?" He gave her no chance to answer. "She's a genius! I think she should get a raise."

Bella sat across from him. "Mark, she's getting an incentive bonus when the case is won. She'll be rewarded then. What has she done that's particularly genius?"

He told her about the patient lists and division among the two of them to take depositions. He'd asked her to do some legal research, which was done in an hour. "This," he said, holding a death certificate, "is genius. She got the certified copies of death certificates of all patients who died while hospitalized. Suicides and accidents. I didn't even ask.

"She's putting notices in the right news media to identify seven or eight patients who were released, but aren't at their last known address to either find them or prove that we made a diligent effort to do so. I love the speech recognition phone system. It's genius. I feel like I have a powerhouse team."

"You do." Bella smiled.

"With one exception."

"There are only two of us. Who's unhappy?"

"Tom. He was displeased, let's say, when I told him about the bugging of his office, conference room/library, and rest room. Even though I pointed out the upgrades and added security, he didn't like being spied on by the AG's office."

"I can't imagine any attorney would. Is he going to leave?"

"He said he'd think about it and let me know within a week. He's a tax attorney. He rarely sees clients or talks on the phone. Most of what he does is online. I doubt anything was compromised."

"Maybe," Bella said. "The IRS computer system is sixty years out of date and is frequently hacked. Tax court has eAccess for cases that are fairly new and supposedly only available to attorneys. I think he's okay. The AG wants to track your activity on the Cooper case, nothing else.

"Were I in his position, I'd be pissed. I'd probably leave, but as you said, he doesn't like the old boys either and he's stuck in Richmond until his wife finishes her residency. I'm sure partners at the big firms routinely spy on their attorneys and support staff."

Mark started to say something. Bella didn't let him. She'd had enough of his defense of the old boys. He still wasn't completely convinced they'd turned on him.

"Use that as a reason for Tom to stay. Tell him everything has been removed, your surveillance has been upgraded, and you now have state-of-the-art communication and computer security. Don't tell him Opal has mad hacking skills."

Mark thought about it.

"You're right. All the law journals are full of articles about firms spying on their associates and even their social media accounts. It's not just Richmond. It's endemic to the profession. I'll make a case for him to stay."

Bella shifted her position to show slightly more leg. She wanted to move on.

"Any peeps from our esteemed adversaries?"

"Not a word. I'm going to the Commonwealth Club for lunch with my father. I want to be highly visible with a respected old boy. They can't shun me there."

"You're getting the hang of this." She projected that lovely bell-like laugh and flipped her hair back over one shoulder. She was in a flirtatious mood.

"Ready for oral arguments Monday?" She hoped the answer was yes. She'd figuratively drawn him a map of impregnable legal arguments.

"I am, indeed. The papers address every aspect of jurisdiction. There isn't a single omission."

Of course not. Bella leaned forward to appear especially interested. "Tell me about the judge. Madeline King." Having hand-picked her, Bella already knew everything there was to know about her, but listening to Mark recite her attributes was pleasant.

Mark didn't hesitate. "Smart. Fair. I don't know how we got her. She's the best of the bunch. All the right credentials. Clerked for United States Supreme Court Justice Sandra Day O'Connor, so she's an open-minded conservative. The best we can hope for."

"What's she like on the bench?" Bella wondered aloud.

Mark thought before he responded. "Courteous. Demands respect. Fines for lateness. Doesn't need her hand to be held to connect the dots. Rhetoric annoys her. Hates visual aids unless they're evidentiary. Moves things along."

All good. Bella nodded. "Does she have a family?"

"A husband who is a philosophy professor at Virginia Commonwealth University. Two kids. A daughter at Smith. A son getting his PhD from MIT in some arcane mathematics field that no one understands."

"Any relatives with mental illness?"

Mark's face fell. "I don't know. You're

wondering if there's anything for which she might have to recuse herself."

"Of course. They're not going to be pleased with an open-minded judge. Ask Opal to check about her family this afternoon. Frankly, I think everyone's family has at least one cousin or uncle or grandparent with mental illness. No reason to demand she recuse herself."

"Worth looking into. You look fantastic, by the way." He stood, righted his tie, and put on his suit jacket. He checked a large gold watch she hadn't seen. "Rolex." He shrugged. "A graduation present I had to wear."

She laughed. "I thought you might be going gangsta'."

"It's coming off as soon as I get back. Gotta go. Can't be late for Dad."

Mark hadn't been gone more than two minutes when Opal walked in with the staff directories at Commonwealth Psychiatric for the past seven years. "There's a lot of turnover even at the top. There have been six chiefs of staff."

"Mmmm," Bella said as she perused the list. "Let's start with the nurses—RNs, BSNs, and NPs. They usually have a good handle on what's going on. Set up depositions for the ones who have retired, resigned, or were terminated first. We'll get subpoenas for current employees."

Opal sat next to Bella on the white leather sofa. "Bella, this is such a cool job. It's like being a spy."

Bella laughed. "It's called legal discovery. Getting information. You never know what might turn up and change the entire case. It's fun sometimes. At least when the surprises are in our favor."

"Why do I think nothing surprises you?" Opal asked.

"It's Friday. I think surprises are over for the week."

CHAPTER FOURTEEN

The downside of the genius phone system was that it required Bella to have a phone. She didn't expect any calls. She was surprised to hear its annoying buzz about eight o'clock Friday night. Mark. She picked up.

"I need you."

"Where?" She forced herself to sound delighted to receive what was either a drunken call or a panic call.

He gave her the address of a college hangout near the Commonwealth Club. She assured him she'd be there soon.

She wore emergency black. Sweater, slacks, and boots. It made her blue eyes even more noticeable and flattered her skin tone. With her blonde hair loose, she was a knock-out. She couldn't recall pulling a drunk out of a bar. Ever. She hoped it was panic.

Mark was hanging on to the black iron rail outside the red brick building in a row of red brick buildings. He looked unsteady, but not drunk. Panic she could handle.

"What's up?" she asked.

"I need help getting home. I drank too much." He spoke clearly. His speech wasn't slurred. Definitely just panic.

"And no one could call you a cab?" She pretended to pout.

"Not anyone I wanted to talk to once I got there."

Taxis didn't regularly cruise the streets of Richmond. The ones that did traveled the circuit of downtown hotels for patrons going to the airport, dinner, or events at the Coliseum. She took out her phone and pressed the app for a cab. The address of their current location popped up automatically. A cab would be there in 6.35 minutes.

She put her arm through Mark's and walked to the corner. She'd get in first. The driver wouldn't see her. He'd only see Mark. She leaned into him and whispered, "No talking in the cab. Security. Remember?"

He put his finger to his lips in a gesture of silence.

The cab arrived, Mark spit out an unintelligible address, and the cab headed south and west. They rode for about fifteen minutes and pulled in front of a row of steel and concrete townhouses. Mark's was on the end overlooking the James River. He gave the driver a fifty-dollar bill and got out. She quickly slid out before he closed the door on her.

"Do you have your keys?"

He held up a sterling silver key ring and an electronic entry card. He walked straight to the entrance, opened it, and entered the enormous first floor that was almost completely empty except for a sleek white kitchen. He didn't move like he was drunk.

"Go upstairs and sit," Bella said.

If Mark noticed that she knew the location of his seating area, he didn't mention it. As with Daniel's home with Selma, Bella had visited Mark's townhouse. She knew the layout of his townhouse and emptiness of his lifestyle. He was a good lawyer for her purposes, but he was immature. He'd lived in a downtown condo near the courthouse where many other single professionals did until two years ago, but most of his neighbors had married, moved to houses, and had children. He'd bought this townhouse on a whim when one of his law school buddies had offered him a chance to get in at a pre-construction price. He had a housekeeper who came once a week who cooked, left meals, and cleaned. Evidently, she hadn't come this week.

"Can you make it on your own? I'll make coffee."

He nodded and started up the stairs. Bella hated being in a kitchen. Fortunately, Mark had one of those cup-at-a-time brewers so she selected Columbian Blend, inserted it, and waited thirty seconds for it to pour. He had white ceramic mugs. She thought about sugar and cream and decided against it. Strong, hot, and black would wake him up. The aroma was pungent. That would help.

The townhouse was huge and empty. What little furniture and wall decor existed was grey, white, and metal with black and white art in metal frames. It read cold. Not how a successful thirty-five-year-old man should live.

She walked up the steps to the second floor and found him sitting in a cushioned wicker club chair on the balcony. She handed him the coffee and sat in the chair next to him. "It's pleasant out here. A nice night."

He sipped the coffee and grimaced that it was black. Right, he liked lattes. Well, given the circumstances, he was lucky to get that. She did her best imitation of charm and concern.

"Have you eaten, Mark?"

"Not since lunch."

"That's quite a while. Do you have anything in the kitchen?"

He laughed. "Whatever the housekeeper brings. This was the model unit. I bought it as is. There was plastic food in the refrigerator."

"Got it," she said. He looked like he'd need a second cup of coffee. She'd look for some crackers and assumed the plastic food was long gone. He finished his coffee in silence and put the cup on the table between them. She picked it up and headed inside. He touched her arm. "Please. Stay."

"I'll be right back with a refill."

When she returned, Bella had coffee and a package of unopened water crackers. It wasn't great, but it would be something in his stomach. She arranged them on a plate. No butter, cream cheese, or dip.

He ate a few crackers and dutifully drank the coffee. She took in the silence and the view of the river and the city on the other side. These were very pleasant surroundings if someone took the time to make a home.

"I'm not drunk. I needed to see you," he said finally.

She'd wait for him to tell her whatever it was.

"I had two drinks at lunch and a couple of beers this afternoon in the bar, where those college kids made me feel ancient and jaded. I took a walk and ended up back there. I had to leave and didn't know where to go so I finally called you." He looked to see if she was listening. "Lunch sucked."

"What happened?" She summoned compassion. She'd already anticipated what had happened.

"Big show. My father put on a great act of having lunch with his only son at one of his clubs surrounded by all his friends. He laughed and shook hands and generally was a jolly good fellow. We had excellent food. No wine. That's for the rare woman guest. We had Scotch before lunch.

"We talked about nothing. He asked about Carlton and Redstone. Wasn't I ready for a new car? Did I really enjoy living on the south side? Had I heard from my sister? We had dessert and coffee. The dining room emptied out and we adjourned to one of the private rooms."

Bella filled in the rest. "Where he got to the real purpose of the lunch, given that no business conversation is allowed in the dining room." She wanted to hurry him along. Attractive as he was, she wanted him to get to the point.

"Right. Withdraw the lawsuit, let the state write the Coopers a check for $250,000 for their drug addicted son's death, and move on to matters more appropriate for someone like me. He'd be glad to make some referrals."

"You were surprised?" she asked. She couldn't help herself.

He looked at her. Then he laughed his Mark crinkly-eyed rich laugh.

"Yes, I was. Unbelievable as it may seem to you, I was surprised. Bugging my office wasn't enough. You were right about the deb. She got a date with a trust fund boy who needs a wife and kids to keep him on the straight and narrow in return for letting workmen into the building. Yes, I was surprised my father was sent to warn me off."

"Duly warned," she said.

He looked her directly in the eyes. He seemed completely sober. He shook his head and looked at her again. "Does nothing surprise you?" he asked.

"I'm sure something will at some point." She smiled.

"I've never met anyone like you. Man or woman."

"I'll take that as a compliment."

"This morning I felt like I was king of the world. The office is secure, Opal is great, we're ahead of schedule. One lunch with my father and I doubt myself. You never doubt yourself, do you?"

She didn't take the bait. He kept talking aloud.

"Of course not. You think things through. You plan. You consider consequences and adjust the plan. Why should you doubt it? You've decided among all the scenarios, the one you picked will most likely work for you."

He stared at her again.

"Something like that." She sat back in her chair,

closed her eyes, and enjoyed the light warm breeze on her face. Fall had yet to arrive.

"When this is over, I think I need to get out of Richmond. I'm thirty-five years old and never lived anywhere else except seventy miles away in Charlottesville. I'm not part of the club anymore. I don't have a family. My sister is in Australia and my parents are here, but not here for me." He sounded like he was testing a theory.

"Get married. Make a family," she said with her eyes still closed.

"What?" He raised his voice. She'd caught him off guard. She opened her eyes and turned in her chair to face him.

"You're thirty-five years old, Mark. Your family should be your wife and children, not your parents."

"Ouch."

"You didn't call me to sit with you because you wanted someone to listen to you. That's not what I do. You know that. You're too smart, handsome, and sexy to be living like a hermit in this cavernous house, working on cases you can handle in your sleep, and doing nothing for fun except some solo sailing. Someone broke your heart along the way. It happens. It doesn't require mourning for however long it's been."

"Eight years. It's been eight years."

"Move on. You've squandered eight years out of thirty-five on her. That's a quarter of your life. How many more years are you willing to give up?"

"I'm a pariah. I broke off an engagement with a deb. I let her say she did it to save face, but everyone knew. It was less than a week before the wedding. Her parents weren't happy. Mine certainly weren't happy."

"You were happy, though. At least not shackled to someone you didn't want. Why the wait?"

"I needed to wait until she found someone else."

Bella burst out laughing. Not her man-tingling laugh. A full-throated from the stomach out of her mouth laugh. "In what universe is that a rule?"

"I'm glad you think consideration for others is funny."

"Oh, please. That's not consideration. That's martyrdom. I'll bet she was married within two years. What's your excuse for the last six?"

"Eighteen months, actually."

"Really, this is none of my business. I'm your colleague on this case. I respect you. I don't want to make it personal." She stood.

He reached up and took her hand. "I do. Bella, I want it to be personal with you."

"I'm not available, Mark," she said softly.

"You know there's something between us."

"That doesn't make me more available. Get some rest. You need to bring your A game Monday." She squeezed his hand. "I'll see myself out."

CHAPTER FIFTEEN

Bella sent Mark a text Sunday night.

Kick Ass.

He didn't respond. He seemed determined to prove he not only knew what he was doing, but could do it alone. Good for him. His spine was showing.

When she invisibly entered the courtroom after proceedings had started, Bella saw that the deputy attorney general was flanked by two associates and three clerks. Mark sat alone at the plaintiff's table. Judge King had called the court to order and the parties had given notice of their appearances for the record.

Mark spoke first. In eight minutes, he summarized the reasons the federal court had jurisdiction over the subject matter of the case and was able to grant the remedy that was requested. That's all the law required. Mark sat.

The deputy AG made a preliminary statement.

An associate started a discourse on the history of jurisdiction. Judge King interrupted.

"We all know the requirements for jurisdiction. There's no need for a history lesson. Do you have anything else to add?"

"No, your honor," said the young woman and sat down.

A second associate was up. He meandered around the question of whether the case met the requirements to be heard in federal court. He ended up repeating Mark's argument.

"You do realize, Mr. Bassett, that you just argued in favor of this court's jurisdiction."

"I apologize, your honor. If it please the court…"

"It doesn't."

The deputy AG attempted to make what they considered to be their primary argument. The federal court didn't have jurisdiction to award the remedy sought by the plaintiffs—$19 million dollars in damages to Evan Cooper's survivors plus $1 million dollars in punitive damages and the closing of Commonwealth Psychiatric Hospital.

"Who would order the closing of Commonwealth Psychiatric Hospital for multiple egregious civil rights violations if not a federal court, Mr. Deputy Attorney General?" Judge King asked.

Unprepared, he stammered it was up to the state legislature.

"I want to be certain I understand your position. A federal court cannot enforce federal civil rights?"

"Not entirely, Your Honor. In this case, there are budget considerations for the state. That's a matter for the state legislature."

"Could you please explain what budget considerations you're referencing. There's nothing in your papers about budgets."

"Your honor, that's an oversight."

"Thank you. You may sit down."

"I've read your papers thoroughly. Mr. Hoffman, I must say your legal memorandum in support of your motion was perhaps the best I've read in my fifteen years on the bench and persuasive. I find in favor of the plaintiff's motion to move forward with this case."

"Notice of Appeal," said the deputy AG.

"So noted. We'll have a scheduling conference next Monday at eleven o'clock. Any questions?"

"No, your honor," stated both Mark and the deputy AG.

"Adjourned."

***

Bella waited and watched a handsome, confident Mark take a few questions from the media outside the courthouse. He answered succinctly and directly with a soupçon of humor. The gaggle of lawyers from the AG's office fled with no comment.

She got to the office midday. Opal was at lunch and Mark was eating a ham on rye sandwich at his desk when she got to the office.

"Congratulations," she said and walked in with a genuine smile. "I saw you on the news at noon. Sounds like you kicked ass and more."

He wiped his mouth with a napkin. "How did I

look?" He teased.

"Confident." She sat in one of the chairs in front of his desk. "Handsome. In fact, you were the most handsome man on the screen."

Mark laughed. "Given that reporters are some of the most bedraggled people in Richmond, I'll still take that as a compliment."

"What did you do to the AG's office? They scurried off like they were terrified of reporters."

"I didn't do a thing. Judge King let them make fools of themselves and promptly ruled in our favor. They're appealing to the Fourth Circuit Court."

"Of course. No doubt hoping some old boy will give them a break."

"You can't let that go, can you?"

Without raising her voice, Bella made her point. "I'm not going to. You may forget how entrenched those old boys are in the legal system, but I don't. They have tendrils in every court. I expect their every move to be calculated to manipulate the outcome in their favor."

He didn't respond. She hoped he recalled how they'd not only bugged his office, but sicced his father on him to drop the case just three days ago. He knew with certainty he was an outsider now, but Mark sometimes acted like a boy who couldn't quite believe he'd been unjustly expelled from the fraternity.

She let him finish eating before bringing up next steps. They'd had a victory this morning, but they had to remain vigilant and keep going at full throttle. "What's next?"

"Depositions." He tossed his sandwich bag into

the wastepaper can with a nice lob. "Opal has scheduled depositions for us for the next two weeks. You're getting former nurses from the hospital and some former patients. I've got former physicians and some former patients. One of us has to depose Larry Yarbrough, aka the Psycho Killer."

She held up her hand. "Please, let's stick to Yarbrough. Psycho Killer dehumanizes him. Don't forget, he was a patient at the time of the murder. What's his mental status?"

"According to the warden at Red Onion, he's unavailable due to illness."

"Red Onion. Is that a joke?" That name hadn't turned up in Bella's research.

"No, my dear New Yorker, that's the name of Virginia's maximum security prison."

Bella knew how little the state valued its only forensic hospital. She wasn't going to pursue the status of its prison system. Red Onion? It sounded like a tavern. "I'm sure he's not getting any treatment. He's probably in solitary. They'd be afraid to allow him in the general population or the infirmary."

"Correct on both counts. I just e-filed a motion to compel assessment, treatment, and deposition. Any evaluation in the transcripts of the murder trial is cold. We need a current assessment of his mental health. Something to support the state's culpability in Evan Cooper's death. One of our three psychiatric expert witnesses can assess him."

"Two experts," she said. "I just saw a notice of appearance for the defense filed by one of our experts on Opal's desk." She expected anger. She saw only a flash of it quickly replaced with all business.

"One down. Whoever it was just disqualified himself from the case for either party."

Mark stood and walked to sit next to Bella in the chair in front of his desk. He held a can of soda in his right hand.

"The best forensic psychiatrist is at Duke. He's our first choice and the AG has just handed him to us. We need to retain him immediately. I'll call him now and draft an agreement that Opal can overnight to him along with Yarbrough's medical records from the trial transcript. "

Bella nodded. "There's very little there. Nothing at all upon his admission to Petersburg. Very little after his arrest and transfer to jail pending trial, the trial, and sentencing. All of it was physical info. Nothing about his mental health."

"I'm sure our psych can read between the lines."

Bella hoped Mark was right.

"Opal asked if we wanted bank statements from the hospital. What do you think?"

At least Mark was considering multiple moving parts. After he'd gotten over thinking the AG wasn't playing dirty, he thought more clearly and acted less impulsively. Good. Still, Bella didn't like Opal having to prompt him into action. He was such a work in progress, even a club girl hostess outpaced him.

"I don't think so. We don't need to prove corruption. We have the certified financial statements they filed. Let someone else follow that trail in the aftermath of its closing," she said.

Mark high fived her. "I like that—its closing."

She smiled one of her Bella smiles. "It does sound good." It would happen. She'd make it happen. "No slacking, though. We need to keep this case tight. We can't pursue tangents. I'm sure the AG will try to send us on some useless excursions."

"What if they try?" He sounded more collegial than pupil now.

"Ignore it. If it's in the form of a motion, we don't oppose. If it's a witness list, we don't object. They think you are working alone with a paralegal. They'll try to bury you in paper."

"They don't know about my secret weapon." He looked at her as he had Friday night.

"And they don't need to know."

He was getting harder to resist. In just a month, he'd moved beyond following her suggestions to formulating good plans. He was unsurpassed in the courtroom. Add that to handsome and crinkly-eyed laughs and he was a nice package. No baggage. No ex-wife or kids.

She reached in her bag and placed a USB drive in his hand. She let her fingers linger longer than necessary when she touched his palm. Excitement surged through her in a way it hadn't in long time.

"My question list for patient depositions. They're tighter than the ones for hospital staff. Assuming the patients meet the criteria for answering questions under oath, they're still people who not only have a mental illness but endured a stay at Petersburg. I don't think we can expect full concentration for more than thirty minutes. More like twenty. Some will be nervous with a court reporter recording their answers. I want to ease in, get what we need, and ease out. We're the good guys."

"That we are." He looked like he was going to kiss her.

Opal interrupted. "You were awesome on the news at noon, Mark. What do I tell reporters wanting interviews?"

Bella let him take the question. It wouldn't hurt. She just didn't want him spending precious time away from the case.

"I'm not available this week. I'll be in court next Monday at eleven. They can talk to me then."

Bella turned to Opal. "Thanks for setting up the interviews. Great idea to pull their employment records. Anticipation is an excellent quality, and you have it."

Opal almost blushed. "Not a problem."

When she left, Mark asked Bella why she wasn't using the conference room in the office for depositions.

"A legal office will spook former employees and most former patients. They'll be more comfortable in modest hotel conference rooms."

"If you decide you want the conference room here, you can have it."

"Thanks. I'll see you tomorrow." She picked up the personnel files Opal had left, slipped them in her bag, and stood to leave.

"A recap tonight at my place? We could catch the evening news and watch me again."

Bella smiled. "Mark, I'm not setting foot in that monastery. Hire a decorator or a professional stager.

Make a home for yourself."

CHAPTER SIXTEEN

Bella had just enough time to review the personnel file on the nurse she was to meet in the afternoon. She'd asked Opal to schedule the ones who had the longest employment history first. She quickly saw that the nurse scheduled for tomorrow morning would be the gem. She'd left for personal reasons after twenty-four years. She'd been paid to leave.

This afternoon's nurse was terminated due to a Reduction in Staff. She'd be interesting as well.

A chime sounded inside her bag. A text from Opal that this afternoon's appointment needed to reschedule later in the week. Bella had the afternoon off. She'd do some shopping.

***

Annette Tandy was an attractive woman in her mid-fifties. She arrived promptly Tuesday morning, accepted water, and had no questions before starting the deposition. She appeared at ease in the hotel conference room Bella had chosen. They sat across a polished table. The court reporter was across the room. Bella led Annette through the introductory questions to establish her identity, qualifications, and work history.

In response to Bella's question as to whether Ms. Tandy had ever witnessed violations of patients' civil rights to adequate medical and mental health treatment in a safe environment, she pulled out two stacks of paper dating back fifteen years. "I kept these," she said, "in case anyone ever had the guts to take a hard look at that place."

"What are these?" Bella asked. She couldn't use any of them as evidence because there was no way to authenticate them to judicial standards, but the contents could lead to exploration of specific incidents.

"Memos, at first. Then when I realized nothing was going to be done, I just wrote a summary at the end of my shifts."

"Ms. Tandy, I'm going to ask you to walk me through various categories and I'll follow up after I've had a chance to read these. Do you mind if I take them with me?"

"No, I want you to keep them," she said decisively.

Bella nodded in acknowledgement and launched into her questions. "Let's talk about a safe environment. In general, did you consider the conditions at Commonwealth Psychiatric to be safe for patients?"

"Absolutely not. Not for the patients or the staff."

"Ms. Tandy, I can only discuss the patients. Could you give me a sense of why you considered the conditions generally unsafe?"

"Not a week went by without the patients beating each other up. Assault, rape, and attempted murder."

Daniel. Daniel was there. Daniel had been vulnerable. Bella didn't allow herself to react. "Did this happen during any particular time or after a particular activity, such as meals or going outside?"

"No, it happened whenever a patient couldn't control his illness and acted out."

"Why couldn't patients control their illnesses on such a regular basis?"

"They were under-medicated or given no medication. They weren't being treated. They were being warehoused."

"That's a very strong statement. Were there segmented populations? According to whether patients were awaiting competency hearings versus serving sentences for NGRI? According to age? According to where they were in their treatment plan?"

"No separation of populations. Not one of those patients had a treatment plan. We just made notes of their behavior and a tentative diagnosis."

"Who do you mean when you say we?"

"The nurses. Three per shift for 130 patients."

"So the diagnoses could have been wrong?"

"Absolutely. They were wrong. I misdiagnosed patients myself. As I became more experienced, I could tell psychosis from bipolar, but I'm not a trained psychiatrist."

"Patients with an incorrect diagnosis wouldn't receive the medication that would actually treat their condition. Is that correct?"

"Yes."

"Without a diagnosis and treatment plan, patients were not given medication to relieve their symptoms and they acted out violently. Is that correct?"

"Yes."

Bella knew it was bad, but she thought worse was to come.

"Of course, patients were under-medicated too. They were usually the victims."

Bella reacted quickly. "Please strike the last statement by Ms. Tandy. We're off the record," she said to the court reporter.

"Ms. Tandy, please wait for me to ask you a question for the record."

"Sorry, I'm angry. I've been angry for thirty years. I'm finally getting to say something. We tried. So many of us tried, but we couldn't get anywhere. No one listened to us. They didn't care about us any more than they cared about the patients."

"Would you like to take a break? Have more water? Anything else to drink?"

She shook her silver-haired head. Ms. Tandy was serious. She'd taken care with her appearance today. She wore a grey dress with matching jacket, a pink scarf, black low-heeled shoes. Her makeup was perfect as was her manicure. She wore only a wedding ring and a watch. In addition to the RN pin she wore on the lapel of her jacket, she wore a second pin that read **"I'm a nurse. What's your super power?"** She was proud to be a nurse.

"I like your pin," Bella said.

Ms. Tandy smiled. "It is a super power. No one knows more about patients than nurses."

"An underappreciated and underpaid profession," Bella remarked.

"Thank you."

"Ms. Tandy, are you ready to go back on the record?"

"Yes."

Bella announced they were on the record and continued her safety questions. She'd then skip to why Ms. Tandy left.

"Ms. Tandy, without a proper diagnosis, were any patients over-medicated in your opinion?"

"Yes. Anyone who didn't speak English was immediately sedated. Young women were usually sedated. Elderly patients were always sedated."

"So, the most vulnerable populations were over-medicated?"

"Correct."

"Aside from misdiagnosis, improper treatment plans, and improper medication, were there any other conditions that you considered to be unsafe?"

"Yes. Repeatedly violent patients were restrained and put in seclusion. One patient I recall was in seclusion for twenty-nine out of thirty days each month. He'd make an appearance on census day. That's the day the patients were counted."

Bella decided she'd follow that up in Ms. Tandy's notes.

"Anything else about safety that hasn't been

addressed?"

"Medical treatment. Patients injured during beatings weren't taken to the ER. We did the best we could, but we had no way of checking for internal injuries or splinting broken bones."

"Anything else?"

"Suicides could have been prevented. We were never told if patients were suicidal so they weren't under surveillance for the first few days of their stay. All of the ones that were later found to be suicidal at intake killed themselves."

Bella was horrified. "All of them?"

"All of the ones I knew about. They're in my notes."

"Ms. Tandy, why did you leave under a settlement agreement?"

"That's supposed to be confidential, but I'm going to tell you. I was disgusted with what they were doing. I compiled a report on every doctor there. I was going to take it to the Professional Licensing Board. One of the aides ratted me out. The next thing I know, I'm sitting in the state's HR in a state office building with a state attorney asking me to sign a document. My privileges at Commonwealth Psychiatric Hospital had been suspended during their so-called investigation into my performance. It was found to be unsatisfactory and my nursing license was going to be revoked. I could never practice in this state again. With a revoked license, I'd never practice anywhere again."

That was both stupid and harsh on the part of the state. "What did they propose as an alternative?" Bella asked.

"I would retain my license. In consideration of my nearly twenty-five years of service, they would pay my regular salary and benefits until I reached the retirement date, accept my retirement application, and pay me $10,000 for any expenses I might have incurred during my investigation."

"What expenses did you incur?" Bella was puzzled.

"None. They thought I'd consulted an attorney. I should have, but I thought the Licensing Board would at least hear me out. They didn't ask for any bills. They just picked $10,000 as the amount I might have incurred and showed me the door."

"I see," Bella said. She hoped this story had a decent ending.

"Where do you work now, Ms. Tandy?"

"I'm the supervising care manager for three private nursing homes owned by the Presbyterian church. My patients and their families get excellent care."

"Thank you, Ms. Tandy. That concludes the deposition of Annette Tandy." Bella stated the date, time, and location once again for the record.

She'd have to tell Opal to reschedule the remaining nurses. She couldn't do three of these per day.

CHAPTER

SEVENTEEN

Bella held back tears.

The years had not been kind to her friend. A slim thirty-five year old was now an emaciated forty-five year old woman who hadn't seen the sun or the inside of a Saks for five years. No matter how she looked, her brain was a sponge for politics. Offered a weekly column after ten years as the lead political correspondent for a network, she knew that meant her over-forty face could only be seen on TV once a week and pre-empted for virtually anything determined to be newsworthy, such as celebrity birthdays.

She launched HUP/dc, a political blog where she followed the news she wanted and made her opinions known. Hollywood for Ugly People/dc started with 35 subscribers and within six months had 40,000. She was a legal junkie. The Supreme Court, appellate courts, county courts. Even tax court. Despite news updates at least every day,

HUP/dc had never once offered a correction or retraction. She was accurate, wicked, and deadly.

Sitting on a bench near the gym at American University, she chain-smoked until her informant arrived.

"Who, what, when, where, and how?" She put her hand out for the USB drive. Bella handed her a manila envelope too.

"Fourth Circuit judge. Owns one-third interest in child pornography network, last ten years, brothels in Las Vegas, New Orleans, and Laredo—that's in Texas. Through a server in Ottawa. Likes to sample the boys and take selfies. Stomach churning and heartbreaking."

"Legit?"

"I was at the scene of the blackmailer's OD."

"In?"

"Nevada."

"When?"

"Two weeks ago. Chalked up as another junkie OD. Cops didn't bother to take the computer holding the treasure."

The blogger blew out a long puff of smoke. "A federal appeals court judge." She shook her head.

"Nothing shocks you." Bella knew this woman was even more cynical than herself.

"This," she said emphatically. "This does. When do I upload?"

"Sunday at eleven o'clock. He goes to mass with his wife. Media should be waiting for him when he comes out of the church. Photographs are always nice, especially since he has a fondness for pictures of himself."

"Done. Gives me enough time to confirm the story."

"As you wish."

"Hey." She put out her cigarette. She looked directly into Bella's eyes. "This is important. No one should mess with kids. Thanks."

CHAPTER EIGHTEEN

October

"Opal, you have no idea how much time you've saved us," said Bella when Opal presented her with a stack of papers representing the minutes of the Local Human Rights Committee monthly meetings. The LHRC was charged with overseeing protection of patients' civil rights at Commonwealth Psych and reported their monthly findings to the State Human Rights Committee. If Mark could show there were abuses at the hospital that the LHRC knew about and didn't correct, then it was reasonable to claim that the state knew. Either the state read and approved the lack of action or didn't read the minutes. Either way, the state had dropped the ball. Drop the mic.

"Printing them took more time than finding them. It's really hard to believe how easy it is to get stuff from the state."

"As I said, Opal, these are public documents but we have to file a request to get them. That request gets shuffled around, temporarily lost, and finally lands on someone's desk on top of two years worth of previous requests. I know you're the best, but they probably have very little security around them."

"None," Opal responded.

"Ah," Bella said. "It's worse than I thought."

"Even these," Opal presented a smaller stack of paper, "weren't protected."

Bella scanned the title. "The closed Executive Sessions that are supposed to be secret?"

Opal nodded.

"Opal, you are a gem. No pun intended." Bella paused. "Do you even like opals?"

"I don't know. I've only seen one as a birthstone ring and it was tiny."

She'd lost some of her defenses. After realizing Mark and Bella really were the good guys in this case and thought highly of her work, Opal had relaxed. She worked with intense concentration and lost almost all her attitude. Her wardrobe was still quirky, but no longer appeared to be a warning signal not to mess with her or an invitation for an anonymous quickie.

"Why don't we go to the Museum of Fine Arts? There's an Australian sculpture exhibit there now. The largest opals in the world are in Australia. We could go and have dinner afterwards. There's always jazz on Saturday nights."

"The museum? Bella, do you only go to stuffy places?"

Bella laughed. Not her man-charming laugh, but still delightful. "There's nothing stuffy about an

Australian anything. You have to eat. Why not do it someplace new? You'll be done in plenty of time to hit the clubs."

"Okay," she said reluctantly.

"Opal, we'll go. If you hate it, you can leave. We have a date for dinner Saturday?"

"Date."

***

Mark pulled Bella into his office late Friday morning. "I've got something to show you," he said. His eyes danced with mischief.

Bella looked around the room. Nothing had changed. No new file folders lying on the desk. No new computer. Still no rug.

"Our opponent surrendered and you had the document framed."

"No, if that happened, the office would be closed and the three of us would be on a plane to Fiji."

"I give up," she said and leaned against his glass-topped desk.

"It's not in the office. I have to take you somewhere to see it."

"Now?"

"Tomorrow night. About ten o'clock."

She purred. Bella quite liked the idea of meeting Mark somewhere mysterious late in the evening.

"I have plans, but I'll be finished by then." She wanted Mark to wonder what her plans were even if they were with Opal. "Where should I meet you?"

"The Jefferson Hotel. It's a charity thing, but I'll be done by ten."

107

"Is this something at The Jefferson?"

"Maybe."

She toyed with him. "Will I be blindfolded?"

"Maybe."

"Will I keep all my clothes on?" Her expression never changed, but Mark's faced flushed.

"Maybe."

"That's an awful lot of maybes. Not a single yes. Is this going to be worth my time?"

"Yes."

"Then I'll meet you at The Jefferson."

CHAPTER NINETEEN

Set against the brocade red and gold velvet furnishings of The Jefferson Hotel lobby, Bella looked demure in a body conscious, champagne just off-the-shoulder cocktail dress and silk sandals. She stood idly by the sweeping staircase that had inspired the famous one in *Gone with the Wind* waiting for Mark. When he started down the steps, he saw her and mouthed, "OMG." He was surrounded by young women in evening clothes that looked like prom dresses or mother-of-the-bride wear. They actually stumbled into each other when they saw Bella.

Mark continued down the stairs and took Bella's hand when he reached the lowest step.

"You really are sex on a stick. Do you realize that dress makes you look completely naked from a distance?" he whispered in her ear and took time to nuzzle her neck.

"No, I had no idea. It's a perfectly conservative dress. I've just come from the museum and no one suggested I was improperly dressed."

He laughed out loud, and his eyes crinkled in the way she loved.

"Mark, you've left your harem behind. They seem to be stuck slack-jawed on the staircase. They can't move. Was this a bachelor auction?"

He laughed again. They reached the parking valet and waited for Mark's car to be brought around.

"If the Richmond newspaper still had a society column, you'd be the hottest topic. Naked mystery woman crashes charity event in the gracious lobby of the venerable Jefferson Hotel."

"Oh, Mark." Bella laughed in delight. "Don't you think that lobby is a bit much? It looks like a bordello. I expect Rhett Butler to scoop up Belle Watling rather than Scarlett O'Hara and carry her to his bed."

The car was brought around, Mark opened the passenger door, and she slid in. He put the top down and she whipped an ethereal chiffon scarf out of her purse to wrap around her hair. They didn't speak during the trip. Once again, Bella found driving so fast and so much over the speed limit to be intoxicating. She wanted to fly down highways forever in a convertible.

They pulled into Mark's garage and he led her into the house.

"I've been here before," she said with exaggerated disappointment.

"That was the before. Now, you'll see the after."

She looked around. In the few days since she had told him to make himself a home, he had. The walls were painted in greys and whites. There was a glass-topped dining room table with seating for eight. The kitchen had small appliances, utensils, and an herb garden on the counter. The rear patio was landscaped with a privacy hedge and furnished with seating for a casual party.

She floated up the suspended staircase to the second floor, which now had a fully furnished living room and two guest bedrooms. The living room had a media center, comfortable leather couches and chairs, and throws tossed over ottomans. Modern paintings and sculpture were strategically placed and lit throughout the house. A framed photo of Carlton's Macho was the single personal touch.

Up another level was the master suite with a sitting area. Everything was designed with flawless contemporary furnishings highlighting the gleaming burled maple furniture and drew attention to the outdoor deck. Again, there was a privacy hedge, but low enough not to obstruct the view of the river and the city. Lounge chairs were strategically placed. The master bath was a spa.

"It's beautiful, Mark."

"No traces of a monastery?" He looked earnest.

"None. A hedonist who does things when he sets his mind to it. One who just needs a push."

Mark pulled her close to him. The smell of him aroused her.

"I know exactly what I want. I want you."

She unbuttoned his top two shirt buttons and ran her forefinger with its scarlet nail down his neck to his chest. She hadn't touched a virile handsome man in ages. Running her fingers along his skin was like catnip to her. She wanted more. Now.

"Do you have on anything at all under that dress?" he asked.

"I don't recall. Why don't you check?" She whispered in his ear. The smell of him was intoxicating.

He unzipped the back of the dress and it fell to the floor. Bella was completely naked down to her Brazilian wax. He moaned as she stood before him. Beautiful, confident, inviting. Her body was both toned and luscious. She wanted him to look at her. Were this not their first time, she could make him climax without touching her. She wanted him. Those hands on her. His mouth. The weight of him. Everywhere.

He yanked off his clothes and she set herself free.

CHAPTER TWENTY

Bella heard Mark moving around in the kitchen while she lounged in bed. The aroma of rich coffee floated from the first floor through the empty space surrounding the stairs to the bedroom. She rolled over and lay on her side. What a delicious lover he was. He'd treated her body with reverence. And desire. And urgency.

He seemed surprised that she'd matched him in every way and willingly followed his lead. She'd decided letting him take the lead was best. She could just relax, but he stirred something in her that made her want to show him he could up his game and she'd be right there with him.

They'd pleasured themselves throughout the night. Whispering occasionally. She'd kept her blue eyes wide open when they climaxed simultaneously. Throughout, she'd been sensuous, erotic, and amorous. She didn't like or want lewd, bawdy, or rough sex. Apparently, neither did Mark. She was surprised he was a skilled lover. He certainly hadn't learned that with a deb. Somewhere

113

in his life, there was a woman who'd known what she was doing.

"You're up early," she said when he came into the room. "It's Sunday. The time for sleeping late, rolling around in bed, and reading the paper in bed."

"What about watching politic talk shows?"

"Please tell me you don't watch those. All that shouting over each other."

"No, I don't." He kissed her. "Bella, last night was like a whole new dimension for me. I've never been loved so thoroughly and sensually."

"Thoroughly? Does that mean we're done? There's nothing left?" she teased.

"We're just getting started."

"Good," she whispered.

"Tell me about that rolling around in bed part of a Sunday morning. I'd like to get the hang of that."

***

Bella was pretending to be in the shower when Mark heard the news about Judge Paul Whiting of the United States Fourth Circuit Court of Appeals. Mark was talking back to the TV in the kitchen. She took her time dressing. She'd had the foresight to bring a change of clothes. She was just applying the final touches of makeup when Mark bounded into the room.

"You've got to see this. Come on." He grabbed her by the hand and raced down one flight of steps to what was now the official living room with beige leather sofas, soft grey walls, and a flat screen TV.

"What's this?"

She saw a camera following Judge Whiting and his wife down the steps of their church. He used what looked like a prayer book to shield his face from reporters as he fled into the back seat of a black sedan with his wife in tow. She looked confused and terrified. Reporters ran after the car, shouting.

Mark couldn't contain himself. "Judge Whiting is a partner in a child pornography ring. Making at least two million in untaxed dollars every quarter. He also apparently likes the boys. HUP/dc published photos of him in his brothels in Las Vegas, Laredo, and some other place."

"Why is he holding a prayer book?" Bella had no idea what congregants carried to mass. The fact that he had something with which to cover his face was disappointing. She'd wanted to see fear in his eyes.

"The story broke at eleven while he was at mass. Reporters were waiting on the church steps when he came out. He may not even know what's going on."

"His poor wife."

"You believe it?" he asked.

Bella looked at Mark with disappointment. Was he never going to get how reprehensible these old boys were? "HUP/dc has never been wrong. Everyone's going to be on this. Probably even more to come. I don't want to watch. It's sickening."

"He's on our appellate bench. They're going to be in chaos. The AG has nowhere higher to go on our case." Mark was excited. His blue eyes were alive, and he looked like a boy who'd just won a lifetime of trips up Space Mountain.

"They've no reason to appeal anything," she said

calmly.

"But they threatened to appeal. It's a toothless threat now."

"Mark, it's always been toothless. Can we turn it off now? I thought we were going to the movies."

He stared at her for what seemed like two minutes.

"You're not surprised. You're not surprised at all."

She shrugged.

"What do you know?" He sat next to her. He wanted more dirt.

"Nothing," she said. "I'd heard some talk."

"And you didn't tell me?" He was dumbstruck.

"Mark, rumors fly all the time. Remember, I don't live in Richmond. I move in different legal circles. About fifty percent of rumors are true. Thirty percent are deliberate defamation. The rest, who knows?"

The landline rang. A law school buddy who'd just heard the news. Mark's cell rang twice while he was on the landline.

Bella decided to leave. Mark wanted and needed to spend the day speculating about what would happen tomorrow at the Appellate Court. Would the judge be impeached, step down, or would this all go away through a messy, stomach-churning investigation?

Bella had no interest. The crucial point was that media attention was now focused on the Appellate Court and not their case. The bonus was that attorneys in the AG's office considered Judge Whiting to be a friend. They might be so rattled, they'd make mistakes in the Cooper case. She counted on that.

She walked down to the first floor and waited for Mark to finish his fourth call. She came up behind him and kissed the back of his neck. "You are so delicious," he said before he turned around.

"Where are you going?" His eyes went wide when he saw she was ready to leave.

"Home, Mark. You need to be in the legal loop today. I don't. I called a cab that should be here in less than ten minutes."

His eyes darkened. "I thought we were going to spend the day together."

"We didn't foresee a legal scandal blowing up in your front yard." She gave him a lingering kiss. "Last night was lovely. I'll see you tomorrow after the scheduling conference."

The cab pulled up and honked.

"Bella, last night was amazing. I want you to stay."

"Not today," she whispered in his ear. "You'll find a way to make it up to me. I won't break."

She walked outside, got inside, and concentrated on being visible long enough for the driver to drop her off somewhere she could disappear.

CHAPTER
TWENTY-ONE

Bella shook off the feeling of revulsion after deposing another longtime nurse at Commonwealth Psych. Each meeting revealed more horrors than she'd imagined. She had to remain detached. Looking at pieces of the puzzle that could be used, discarded, or put aside for now, the case made itself.

When she returned to the office, Opal was concentrating on her screen. They exchanged quick waves and Opal looked back at her monitor. She seemed intent on unearthing something. Mark, once again, was eating a sandwich at his desk. He smiled when she walked in.

"You look pleased with yourself," she said as she sat on the sofa. "Come sit."

He picked up a tall Styrofoam cup of iced tea and moved to sit next to her. "I am pleased. Trial starts in eight weeks. We have an order compelling the transfer of Larry Yarbrough to the acute psychiatric unit at Duke's primary hospital with the expectation he can be lucid enough for a deposition. Subpoenas for the current staff at Commonwealth Psych have been served."

"You had a busy morning."

"No. Just me and Judge King. No one from the AG's office showed. Judge King waited fifteen minutes and proceeded without them."

"No one showed up? Not even a lowly first-year associate?" Bella was surprised. The exposure of Judge Whiting's crimes was more useful than she'd anticipated.

"No one. I'm told the most senior people are huddled, speculating about what's up with Judge Whiting. No one else looked at the calendar. I'm sure ours wasn't the only court date they missed."

Bella had never experienced such irresponsibility by her opponent. "Truly? The AG's office missed court dates to their detriment to gossip about a child molesting judge? Are they planning who to nominate to take his place?"

"Most likely, they're considering impeachment."

"What planet are they on? Do they not realize this is beyond their control? This is all going to come down through the feds. A United States attorney for Las Vegas, New Orleans, or Laredo will arrest him in a matter of days or hours for child pornography, if not trafficking in children."

Mark grimaced. The sensationalism from yesterday had disappeared. He now projected the same repugnance she felt for the man.

Good. Her plan was working. The AG's office was making enormous, almost unethical, mistakes due to their preoccupation with Judge Whiting.

"What about Larry Yarbrough's transfer to Duke?" she asked to change the subject.

"Judge King ordered he be transferred, assessed, treated, and deposed forthwith. He's being transferred to Duke this afternoon by ambulance accompanied by federal marshals. The AG's office didn't oppose the motion. I doubt they even read it.

"Dr. Constantine will see him tonight. He said correctional patients usually need one or two days to recover from transfers, but he doubted that would be the case for Yarbrough. He'll be heavily sedated for transport and may only notice he's in a hospital rather than a cell. Constantine said he'll have a preliminary assessment within the next two to three days.

"There's a high probability that Yarbrough's deposition may be considered a dying declaration. According to Constantine, a longtime bath salt user who undergoes sudden and absolute withdrawal will exhibit drastic physical deterioration. Psychiatric treatment may not have a chance to reach therapeutic levels if Yarbrough's physical condition is poor. Constantine knows we need Yarbrough on the record and will work toward that goal in addition to treatment."

"Oh, that's grim." She looked away from Mark and down to recover herself. "Even I don't want to think this was calculated by the state, but it's withheld medical treatment since Yarbrough was arrested for Evan Cooper's murder. That's one of the most basic civil rights for a patient. The state is killing him by doing nothing."

Mark cupped her chin and tilted her face to see

her. "Hey, where did my hard-charging, take no prisoners legal barracuda go?"

She put her head on his shoulder. "She's there. She has to take moments now and then to transform her revulsion at what humans inflict on each other into anger. She needs a break."

She would've been content to spend the afternoon exactly as she was. Held by a good guy who wanted to right wrongs.

Opal yelled from the hall.

"Turn on the TV. Mrs. Whiting just shot her husband on the courthouse steps."

Mark grabbed the remote and turned on the TV. Tom joined Mark, Bella, and Opal in watching the assassination unfold. Footage of a distraught woman in her fifties wearing a bathrobe while screaming and firing an automatic pistol at the judge was on loop. Five. Six. Seven shots. Her shouts were barely audible, but the words children, husband, and pervert were repeated. She was easily taken to the ground by court police.

A jerky camera cut to where Judge Whiting lay face forward on the steps of the Italianate Lewis F. Powell, Jr. United States Federal Courthouse. The camera captured only a pool of blood above his neck. Blood poured down the four shallow concrete steps onto the brick sidewalk. There was no pedestrian traffic. People must have fled to avoid being in the line of fire.

Another camera angled on the EMS team, who rushed to where Judge Whiting lay sprawled. He was quickly placed on a stretcher, loaded into an ambulance, and driven away with sirens blaring.

Two Richmond police officers moved forward to cover the scene with a tarp. Other officers blocked off the street and rerouted traffic.

A young man who was covering the court for the day appeared on screen in a borrowed suit jacket two sizes too large and a half-knotted tie. The wind blew it into his face until he used one hand to hold it down and the other to hold the mic.

"At approximately 1:10 this afternoon, Judge Paul Whiting of the Fourth Circuit Court of Appeals was shot in the back of the head and body by a woman firing an automatic pistol. Judge Whiting had taken his usual daily stroll around the grounds of the State Capitol across the street during lunch and was returning to the courthouse. We have no information on his condition.

"Judge Whiting was the obvious target because the woman ran closer to him as she fired. Court police subdued the woman, removed her weapon, and took her into custody. Police have not released her identity.

"Bystanders took to Main and Tenth Streets to crouch behind parked cars in order to avoid the gunfire. One man, thirty-one-year-old messenger Roger Balsam, witnessed the shooting."

With the mic shoved at him, Mr. Balsam articulated what happened. "I was headed to the courthouse to drop off documents for the clerk when I saw a woman wearing a pink bathrobe at the corner start running toward Judge Whiting as soon as he crossed the street from the Capitol grounds. From what I saw, the first shot hit the back of his head. Every shot after that hit him, too. It was like she was on a mission to kill him."

"Did she say anything?" asked the reporter.

"She was screaming. The only words I could make out as she got closer were married and pervert. Then the police took her down."

"Did you fear for your life?" The young reporter asked. To Bella, the question was an obvious attempt to get a career-making sound bite.

"No. The shooter was clearly aiming for the judge. She wasn't a crazy shooting up the streets. She wasn't a terrorist."

"Thank you, Mr. Balsam."

Mark muted the TV. "I've got to sit down."

"Put your head between your knees," Opal instructed as she got him a glass of water. "Are you okay, Mark? Tom?"

"Yes," they both said.

Tom headed back to his office. Bella asked Opal to sit with Mark. Bella sat at Opal's computer and searched for news updates. She silently screamed, "YESSS!" If she still lived in human form, she'd have done the same thing out loud.

CHAPTER
TWENTY-TWO

By late afternoon, the story had unfolded. Opal, who had been riveted by the details, updated Bella and Mark before she went home.

Warrants for the arrest of Paul Whiting had been served at his home on River Road in Richmond's West End by United State's Attorney Offices in Nevada and Texas. The charges included child sexual assault, creation and distribution of child pornography, sexual trafficking in children, and tax evasion. Warrants to search the home were executed by the Federal Bureau of Investigation.

Mrs. Whiting had been eating breakfast on a tray in her bedroom at the time of service and search. Opal made it clear the judge slept in another bedroom. When Mrs. Whiting read the charges, she understood what her husband had done.

She'd taken her registered pistol, driven to the courthouse, and shot and killed her husband of thirty-seven years. She was being held for observation at Virginia Commonwealth University Hospital—the same hospital where her husband had been pronounced DOA. No charges had been filed yet against Mrs. Whiting.

"There's a lot of noise about Judge Whiting's career and condolences from various public officials. Not as many as I would've thought. Maybe they're trying to decide if condolences for the judge are the right thing to offer publicly."

"Thanks, Opal. Why don't you go home? I'm going to leave early." Mark looked at Bella. "I can't believe I'm saying this, but I'm going to have dinner with my parents. My mother and Margaret—Mrs. Whiting—know each other. They serve on committees together. Dad, of course, knew the judge. Didn't like him, but knew him."

"It's a nice gesture," Bella said quietly.

"Will you stay with me tonight? Wait for me at home?" His eyes searched hers.

"Yes. I'll be there." He dropped his house keys in her hand and left.

***

Bella staged herself to be the comforting presence waiting at home. She wore a silk lounge set, lightly sprayed one of her favorite scents behind her ears and on her wrists, and arranged herself languidly on the sofa in the sitting room off the bedroom. A gas fire was burning. The bar was fully stocked.

When Mark came upstairs, he looked tired. He made himself a scotch, sat next to her on the sofa, and held her hand. "Man, that was grueling."

She waited until he was ready to talk.

"I was stunned Mom had it together enough to make some calls this afternoon. Maybe the shooting happened before she started drinking, although it was after one o'clock. She spoke to both of the Whiting's children, Anna and John. Anna hadn't been allowed to see her mother in the hospital. Margaret's priest was with her and that's all the United States Marshals would allow.

"John was shattered between the revelations about his father, his father's death, and his mother's role in it. He asked Mom if she knew of a service that would right the house after the search warrants had been executed. He'd looked inside the house quickly and fled. Everything was in shambles. The furniture was still upright, but the contents of all the drawers, cabinets, and shelves had been swept onto the floors. His mother couldn't return to the house as it was if she was released. Surprisingly, Mom knew who to call and did.

"Dad said the United States Attorney here is considering not pressing charges given the passionate nature of the crime. In less than twenty-four hours, everything Margaret believed about her husband was proven to be false. She killed the judge immediately after FBI agents appeared with arrest warrants and began tearing the house apart."

"What about the cooling off theory given that she took the time to find and load her gun, drive downtown, and ambush the judge?" Bella asked.

"There's some debate. That's why she's in a hospital under observation rather than a jail cell.

According to Dad, there's strong sentiment that she did everyone a favor and saved the district the embarrassment of a disgraced judge, trials for repugnant crimes in at least two different jurisdictions, and removing him from office. There's little interest in the standard procedure of arresting Margaret and letting her raise an affirmative defense. The sticking point is she murdered a federal official. It wasn't the usual domestic murder."

"She could stretch it to defending her property. She may have thought with him dead, the FBI would go away."

He yawned. "I can't think anymore. I don't want to think about them."

"What do you want?"

"A shower, a massage, and long, slow, wet sex."

"Great, I'll get in the shower and you get the massage oils ready. I'd love a good massage."

Mark laughed and crinkled his eyes. "You know that's not what I meant. On second thought, let's skip the shower and massage." He pulled her to him.

CHAPTER

TWENTY-THREE

Bella had a tough week ahead of her, including LouLou's deposition. Before that, she'd promised Mark she'd be in the office for a conference call with Dr. Constantine after his initial assessment of Larry Yarbrough. She arrived just as it was starting.

"I don't have any remarkable findings about Mr. Yarbrough," Dr. Constantine said. "I'll email a report, but my assessment is that he has Borderline Personality Disorder. That diagnosis is exclusionary. He's not bipolar or schizophrenic or narcissistic or any of the spectrum illnesses.

"My opinion is that he's addicted to bath salts. The precise compound in his current toxicology analysis will be in my report. He was on bath salts when he was admitted to Commonwealth Psychiatric and when he killed Mr. Cooper. Sadly, no one analyzed the amount and composition of the drug he was on at the time of the murder."

Of course not. The state just wanted to arrest, try,

and toss him away.

"Dr. Constantine, what exactly are bath salts?" Bella asked. She'd never used drugs, and she'd never encountered anything stronger than cocaine and heroin in her legal career when she was alive. The stronger drugs probably hadn't been invented before 9/11.

"The short answer is a cheap synthetic recreational drug. Attempts to ban some of the ingredients earlier this decade did little to reduce its availability. Bath salts are highly addictive and cause great physical and mental impairment with prolonged use. The physical effects are heart attacks, hypertension, kidney disease, liver disease, and brainstem herniation, which is fatal. Users are paranoid, violent, and agitated. They're insomniacs.

"Examples of behavior exhibited by those using bath salts may be profuse sweating and body overheating. Users tear off their clothes in an attempt to cool themselves. Euphoria and paranoia provoke aggression, uncontrollable violence toward others, and suicide. Traditional methods of restraint such as commands to stop or the use of pepper spray and tasers are ineffective."

Bella and Mark exchanged looks. When Yarbrough was on them, he must have been uncontrollable. Now, his physical health was compromised.

"I see," Bella said. "Sorry to interrupt. Please continue."

"Not a problem. As attorneys in this case, you'll want a good understanding of the drug. I'll include a detailed summary of the drug in my report today so you'll know exactly how Mr. Yarbrough was influenced. I'll, of course, be the expert on the drug as well as its effects on Mr. Yarbrough."

Mark poked Bella's shoulder before she could roll her eyes or say something Constantine could hear. He knew she disliked doctors, but she hated that they considered themselves gods. Well above mere lawyers in terms of intellect and prestige.

"Mr. Yarbrough's current problems are both medical and psychiatric. He's undergone withdrawal, has extremely strong cravings for the drugs, and his physical health is deteriorating rapidly based on my examination compared to that prepared at the time of the murder.

"My examination as well as his medical records indicate he received no treatment at the Virginia prison. Consequently, his liver and kidneys are severely compromised. He should be on dialysis. He has hypertension and is at high risk for a cardiac event. He receives no cardiac medication. The only medication he receives is an inadequate dose of the sedative Midazolam.

"He's in solitary confinement for twenty-three hours each day. He's restrained when served a meal. I don't like to give a prognosis, but I would be surprised if he survives as long as six months."

Both Bella and Mark were silent as they digested the information.

Bella allowed Mark to take the lead with the doctor. He'd need to know how Dr. Constantine proceeded and why.

"Is he treatable?"

"To some extent. His physical deterioration can't

be reversed, but his symptoms from long-term use of bath salts can be treated."

"Sufficiently enough for him to give a deposition?" Mark asked.

"In an appropriate facility with clinicians familiar with the addiction."

"Dr. Constantine, can you comply with the court order compelling Mr. Yarbrough to be treated and made available for a deposition?"

"I don't make promises. I can comply with treating him. Some of his psychiatric symptoms may be lessened by treatment of his physical health. Certainly, treatment for his cardiac conditions would reduce agitation. Dialysis will improve kidney function but have little, if any, effect on his psychiatric state."

Mark watched as Bella turned on her disarming charm. "Forgive me, Dr. Constantine, but is Mr. Yarbrough conscious? Does he speak?" Too bad Constantine was missing the batting of her lashes.

"He has lingering sedation from the transfer. My observation is that concentration is good for two- to three-minute intervals. He has significant memory loss. He was unable to tell me why he was in prison."

Mark followed up. "Dr. Constantine, we can draft a bare bones deposition that shouldn't take longer than ten minutes if you'll swear to basic facts such as date, time, and his medical condition. He'd have to be lucid enough to understand he's answering questions under oath. Do you think he could become healthy enough for a ten-minute question-and-answer session?"

"Possibly. Everything depends upon how well Mr. Yarbrough responds to medical treatment. Make no mistake. Mr. Yarbrough is a very sick man. He could die tonight or regain mental capacity with successful treatment of his most severe physical symptoms."

Tonight. Time was running out.

"Dr. Constantine, then plan to treat him under the court order," Mark said. "If you have any indication that he is dying, call me and I'll get there for a dying declaration about the murder. If I don't make it, your staff is aware of how to record such a declaration, correct?"

"Certainly."

"Thank you, Dr. Constantine. I look forward to your status reports."

The phone call ended.

"Bella, we might not get what we need from him. He sounds like he's in bad shape."

Bella turned away to compose herself before speaking. "He's in the hands of the best doctor and hospital we could identify. We can't control life and death. We have enough to prove the state's culpability in the murder. Nothing. Nothing changes the fact that a man in his condition shouldn't have been placed in an unsupervised setting with a teenager in detox."

"Sucks," Mark said.

***

Although Bella had kept an eye on her when LouLou was being so obstinate about letting Daniel into her life, the two had only met once. Bella had accompanied her in the ambulance to the ER after the car accident that sent Gregg away and stayed until LouLou's uncle arrived. Bella had declined to see her when she was born. LouLou probably didn't remember their only meeting.

In order to make this proceeding as easy as possible for LouLou, Bella reserved a conference room in a downtown hotel for the day. The hotel was close to where LouLou lived and offered a courtyard view. LouLou was scheduled to arrive thirty minutes prior to the deposition and the appearance of the court reporter who would record the proceedings. Bella wanted her to have time to adjust to her surroundings.

She'd made the room comfortable for LouLou. There was light from a large window overlooking an expanse of green, two buckets filled with large chunks of ice, and a sofa should LouLou need to lie down. There was plenty of fresh fruit and healthy snacks. Bella had the telephone number for LouLou's psychiatrist. The hotel doctor was on standby. An aide would drive LouLou to the meeting. Stress was one of the factors that could precipitate a psychotic episode for the young woman with schizophrenia.

Bella knew LouLou Fleming was not healthy. The death of her father two years ago followed six months later by the loss of her boyfriend Gregg had rocked LouLou's world. She had once been a vivacious, sought-after DJ and performer traveling around the world. Now she only left her loft for scheduled walks. An aide visited every day to ensure that her medication and injection schedules were followed. LouLou saw her psychiatrist once a week. A neighborhood couple delivered regular healthy meals.

Mark had told LouLou his colleague would be taking the deposition. Bella didn't want to ambush LouLou, so she sent a text the day before to let LouLou know she was the colleague. She also reminded LouLou that she could be subpoenaed if she didn't give her deposition voluntarily.

Bella wore her customary black silk Armani suit with black stilettos. Her long blonde hair draped loosely around her shoulders. She couldn't do more to make herself neutral. Bella was a natural beauty with enormous blue eyes. Bella didn't like LouLou's precarious mental state. She liked being in control and was wary of what might set LouLou off. The last thing Bella wanted was to precipitate some sort of episode for LouLou.

Bella barely recognized the woman who entered the conference room. Not only was she underweight and listless, she'd cut her hair into a disheveled short style with heavy bangs that emphasized the darkness around her blue eyes. She wore an orange backless dress that highlighted a tattoo of a rising phoenix on her back that had been shot by a renowned fashion photographer for his final show in Paris two years ago. The dress might once have hugged her body, but now hung loosely on her frame and emphasized her collarbones.

Bella deliberately didn't rise when LouLou walked in the room so as not to frighten her. Even so, LouLou looked like she was going to bolt. Her eyes searched the room as if identifying the exits, she didn't close the door behind her, and she remained standing.

"Hello, LouLou. Please sit. I'll get you some water with ice."

Reflexively, LouLou sat.

Bella poured water, sat the crystal glass on the table in front of LouLou, and returned to her seat across the table. She took a good look at the woman who was her daughter. Although LouLou had large blue eyes, they were disproportionate to her face. Her gaunt face made her eyes look abnormal and her face disfigured. Her hair could have used some highlights. She might be pretty if she didn't look so desperately ill. When LouLou lifted her glass, Bella noticed beautifully drawn tattoos on her hands and arms.

"LouLou, you have beautiful hands. I can see why you'd want to have them inked. I especially like the feather and the barn owl."

LouLou put the glass down and hid her hands in her lap under the conference table. "What about the barn owl?"

She hadn't meant to stumble into weird territory, but she had. Bella kept her voice level and calm. "I know they're striking birds and monogamous, which is rare for any species."

LouLou glared at her. "How do you know that?"

"I grew up in Virginia, LouLou. I know about local flora and fauna. I meant nothing more than to compliment your art and choice of subject."

LouLou stared back, but remained silent for a good five minutes. Bella could almost see the possibilities running through LouLou's head.

"Why are you doing this?" LouLou finally asked. She seemed bewildered more than angry.

"I'm Mr. Hoffman's colleague on this matter. I know your psychiatric history and understand your unease."

"I mean, why are you on this case?" LouLou shifted in her chair as though she were trying to find a comfortable position.

"I want that hellhole in Petersburg shut down forever. It ruins lives. It causes irreparable damage. No one is served by being a patient there." Bella struggled to maintain a calm tone. She was outraged that such a barbaric institution could exist in the twenty-first century. Every basic civil right was violated there and no one in the state cared.

"But you're a ghost. How can you go to court?" Again, the look of perplexity.

Bella smiled. "I won't. I'm writing the motions and briefs and strategizing with Mr. Hoffman. He's smart enough, but he doesn't think outside the box. He might win a modest sum for the family of Evan Cooper, but he won't get the place condemned."

"Why do you care about Petersburg?" LouLou barely spoke above a whisper.

Bella looked at her kindly. "I'm surprised you have to ask. Daniel went there for what was supposed to be three months and ended up staying far too long. He was frightened into catatonia. He went back when he became overzealous in wanting to see you. He was there at the time of the murder of Evan Cooper. Daniel could have been Larry Yarbrough's victim. And you, my daughter, have been there three times. The last stay was so bad you were transferred to a private mental health facility at the state's expense."

"Don't call me your daughter," LouLou said quietly.

"What should I call you? You're the child I let the Flemings adopt when I was a young student at the Sorbonne. Daniel is your father. Just between us, darling. *Entre nous.* Otherwise, I'll call you LouLou or Ms. Fleming."

"I'm a year older than you," LouLou said tersely. "We look the same age. In two years, five years, ten years I'll look older than you. How can you expect to be believed as my mother?"

"I won't be here in two years. Once I get what I want, I'll leave."

Finally, Bella had LouLou's attention.

"You can do that? Go away voluntarily?"

"Of course. Ghost exists because our human lives were cut short. We exist to get what we want and move on."

"You plan to get what you want in two years?"

"Absolutely. I always get what I want. There were a few bumps along the way in this situation, but victory is in sight."

"And then you move on?" LouLou's voice was a mixture of excitement, hope, and relief.

Bella didn't feel slighted by LouLou's obvious eagerness for Bella to move out of her life. There was no fond emotion between mother and daughter. LouLou had a family and it didn't include her. Or Daniel. Bella recognized a deeply buried curiosity in LouLou, but it would have to wait. She wanted to get through the deposition before LouLou tired or lost focus.

"Darling, I'm happy to discuss ghost behavior with you some other time."

LouLou stared at Bella. She must have seen the woman who was her mother clearly for the first time. "You really are gorgeous," LouLou said.

Bella smiled. She was accustomed to people praising her looks. "LouLou, you're lovely."

LouLou made a noise of disgust. "Thankfully, I was spared a lifetime of growing up lovely compared to my exceptionally beautiful mother. I'm glad I was adopted."

"I am too, LouLou. I believe the Flemings were wonderful parents."

LouLou didn't respond. Bella took that as a cue to focus on the reason for their meeting.

"Let me tell you about your deposition. I'll ask questions and you must respond truthfully. Please be brief. If I want clarification, I'll ask follow-up questions.

"The purpose of your deposition is to give a patient's view of the quality of health care in general, psychiatric care, and administration. *C'est tout.* You're not considered an expert witness so your opinion is the only thing we want.

"Did you take your meds this morning? Eat?"

LouLou nodded.

"If, at any time, you don't feel well enough to continue the deposition just tell me. We'll take a break."

LouLou nodded again. "How long will this take? I like to nap in the afternoons."

"You'll be home in time for your nap."

"That's not what I asked. How long?"

Bella was pleased she'd gotten a rise out of her. She'd begun to think LouLou was too placid to understand and respond to questions. "An hour at most. Ready?"

LouLou nodded.

"Then I'll call the court reporter in and we'll get started."

CHAPTER TWENTY-FOUR

After the preliminary questions of name, location, and birth date, Bella got right to the point. "Ms. Fleming, are you on any medication?"

"Yes."

"What are the names and dosages of each medication."

LouLou dutifully responded. She clearly had them memorized.

"Did you drink alcohol this morning?"

"No."

"Did you take a sedative?"

"Yes. Four milligrams of alprazolam."

"Does that interfere with your ability to understand and answer questions truthfully?"

"No."

"Are you under the influence of any other substance—supplements, recreational drugs, prescription medications not written for you?"

"No, no, and no."

Bella hid a smile. "What is your psychiatric diagnosis?"

LouLou responded as if by rote. "I have schizophrenia with psychotic episodes, generalized anxiety disorder, and paranoia."

Bella walked LouLou through the crimes committed for which she was sentenced, dates of her hospitalizations at Commonwealth Psychiatric, and the age she was at each admission.

"You were there to regain competency to stand trial. Were you housed exclusively with others waiting for competency hearings?"

"No."

"Were you housed with inmates who had committed crimes but were found Not Guilty by Reason of Insanity?"

"NGRI?" LouLou took a moment to recognize the full name for what she knew only as an acronym. "Yes."

"Was there any way to tell the difference between those of you awaiting competency determination and those who were serving a sentence?"

"I don't understand the question." LouLou looked confused. She started to chip at some neon orange nail polish on her unkempt hands. Otherwise, she sat perfectly still and ramrod straight.

"Did you wear a different color uniform or badge or wristband that would distinguish you from those serving sentences?"

"No. We all wore the same thing."

"During your most recent hospitalization, had

there been any change made to distinguish the two types of patients? Between the time you were nineteen, twenty-six, and thirty."

"No."

Bella led her through questions about safety, assault, and weapons.

"Who distributed your medications?"

"Whatever clerk was on duty. All of us lined up at different times and got our meds."

"Did you always get the same medication?" Bella kept her voice soft and even. LouLou looked pained.

"No."

"Because your doctor had made changes in your medication?"

"No. The clerk handed us whatever he thought we were supposed to get or were pre-packaged by the shift before. I knew what my meds looked like. Sometimes, I got the wrong meds for three or four days in a row."

"Did you complain?"

"Not after the first time."

"Why not?"

"The clerk threatened to withhold all my meds if I didn't take what he gave me that day. I realized other patients never questioned the clerks."

"Did the clerks who dispensed your anti-psychotic medication wear any designation that he had medical or pharmaceutical training? Such as a name tag that read RN, MD, or RNP? A lab coat that read Pharmacist or Pharmacist Assistant?"

LouLou laughed. She almost went into a fit of giggles. She took a long drink of water and composed herself.

"Please answer in words so the reporter can record your answer."

"Absolutely not. Anyone from the staff could be assigned pharmacy duty." Bella moved as fluidly as she could. She didn't want LouLou to get bogged down or obsessed with one topic.

"Was your treatment affected by receiving the wrong medication?"

"Sometimes." LouLou didn't elaborate.

"Please explain that."

"Some of us knew what color pills we got. Capsule versus tablet. Shape. We'd trade to get the right ones. One guy always had a bunch of pills so if we couldn't trade, we'd get them from him."

"Was this man a member of the staff?"

"No. He was a patient."

"Did you pay this man to get the correct medication?"

"No."

"Did he ever tell you why he would hoard pills and dispense them without asking anything in return?"

"Kind of." LouLou's hands had started to shake. She seemed nervous that she might say the wrong thing.

"Please continue. Take your time."

"He'd been there a long time. He knew how screwed up things were. He was a nice guy who wanted to help make the place less awful." LouLou seemed to have run out of breath.

Bella waited one full minute before suggesting a break. Bella sat back. The court reporter left the room.

***

Bella didn't linger after the break. She could tell that LouLou was tiring.

"One last question, Ms. Fleming. Do you recall a specific incident or incidents where someone might have died for lack of medical care?"

"Yes," she responded without hesitation. "During my most recent time there."

"Could you briefly describe what happened?"

"Some of us were sitting in the day room. I was waiting to see my doctor. A patient suddenly grabbed his chest and passed out. Big pushed the panic button and then picked up High Life—that's what I called the man who'd had a heart attack—and took him to his room. He shouted for me to follow. Big broke the glass where the oxygen canister was stored and gave it to me to get ready for the patient. Big told me to keep High Life warm so I put a blanket over him.

"Big pulled up the rails of the bed, unlocked the wheels, and ran toward the ER pushing the bed. I followed and gave High Life the cannula for oxygen. Big gave him an aspirin to swallow and something else to put under his tongue. We ran down two corridors, through the concourse, and all the way to the ER. Big pushed him through the doors and right up to a doctor. He told the ER doc what he'd done and we left."

Things were worse than she thought. This man would have died without Big and LouLou.

"Do you know Big's name?"

"No. He's been there every time I've been hospitalized. He's the one who always has the right meds."

"Do you know High Life's name?"

"Dan Ramsay," LouLou said without emotion.

Daniel. Bella was horrified. Her Daniel had almost died of natural causes. That could never be allowed to happen. She and Daniel couldn't spend eternity together if he died naturally.

Bella's face remained impassive as thoughts raced in her mind. She hadn't been vigilant enough. Maybe she shouldn't wait until Daniel was healthier to move toward eternity. Heart disease ran in Daniel's family. His father had died of a heart attack, but he'd been in his seventies. Had Daniel really had a heart attack? Maybe it was panic and LouLou didn't understand the difference.

Bella marshalled her thoughts to LouLou's deposition. She wanted it to be complete and over.

"Ms. Fleming, did you pass any medical staff on the way to the ER?"

"No."

"When you returned to the day room, was there any medical staff there? Did anyone mention medical staff responding to the panic button call?"

"No and no."

"This concludes the interview. Thank you, Ms. Fleming." Bella announced the date and time for the record.

Bella was surprised to be the one shaking.

On her way out, LouLou stopped beside Bella's chair.

"Did you mean what you said about ghosts?" LouLou asked shyly. Bella hoped she looked encouraging. "That you would talk to me about ghost behavior?"

"Yes, any time you'd like. You have my number."

CHAPTER

TWENTY-FIVE

Bella was not impulsive by nature. She was brilliant, calculating, and aware of the effects of her considerable charm. She rarely made mistakes. Never in business. Never in love. Once, an oversight in birth control produced LouLou, who was promptly adopted into an appropriate Parisian home. She allowed herself one mistake.

Her Achilles heel was Daniel Ramsay. She'd felt his pull without reservation when they met at age seventeen. For the next five years, they'd been lovers, allies, and confidants. Neither could imagine a life without the other. There was no question they'd be together through eternity.

Where Bella was open to any and all possibilities life offered, Daniel preferred a predictable path and stubbornly defended it. He served as a check on her sometimes overly ambitious fantasies. She drew him into the world of broadened opportunities he would otherwise have left unexplored. They were perfect together.

Until. Until Daniel's eagerness to enter the business world led him to an MBA program in Miami rather than a gap year in Europe with her. She knew he'd be unhappy in Miami and would join her after his first semester, if he lasted that long. She hadn't counted on a pregnancy that would distract her from wooing him and eliminate the possibility of her flying to Miami to convince him over the Christmas holidays.

Without her regular physical presence, Daniel remained in Miami. Bella ended their relationship via letter. She didn't want him to come in the spring, when the baby would be born and by then, her focus and opportunities had shifted. She longed for him, but accepted the fact that her life would be without Daniel.

Their affair seven years ago reminded both of them what a deep and rare connection they shared. Daniel was on the verge of leaving his younger wife when his father died. Always a sentimentalist, Daniel broke down and lost his nerve. Worse, he'd failed to tell Bella he couldn't leave his status quo.

She wouldn't have minded postponing his divorce. In fact, she'd encouraged him not to divorce. She didn't need to be married to him to know he loved her with all his being. She could have waited out his grief, but his cowardice in not telling her of the change in plans infuriated her. She planned and got her revenge.

Still, she'd never stopped loving Daniel. To learn from LouLou that indifference and neglect at Commonwealth Psych could have led to his death by natural causes and eliminate any possibility of their being together forever shocked her soul.

After LouLou's deposition, Bella called Opal and got the date of Daniel's ER visit at Commonwealth Psych as well as the name of the doctor on duty that day. One phone call later, Bella learned that same man was working today. She headed to Petersburg.

***

Still dressed in her black suit and stilettos, Bella walked through the wall into the bleak utilitarian office of Dr. Arnold Moore. He was an ordinary man in every way. Average height, weight, amount of hair. He wore a lab coat with a mustard stain on the breast pocket over an ill-fitting brown suit with scuffed white sneakers. The ego wall in his office where framed diplomas and certificates hung was more akin to a dullard wall. Mediocre state schools, low ranked residencies, and no clinical board certifications. He was a hack.

Of course he was sitting in his office instead of seeing patients. If he was the kind of doctor who didn't respond to a panic call, she doubted he'd voluntarily spend time with patients. He was staring at the computer screen without typing or using the mouse. Watching a movie, no doubt.

Bella waited until he noticed her. He looked at her through smudged eyeglasses. She doubted he could see her clearly.

"Who are you?" He smirked. No doubt anyone who didn't wear a lab coat wasn't worthy of his time and attention.

"Were you on duty when Daniel Ramsay had a heart attack?" she demanded.

"Who are you?" he repeated.

She moved around his desk and closer to his chair. She spoke in a deadly whisper. "I don't like to repeat myself."

Flustered, Dr. Moore moved his hands with grime encrusted fingernails to the computer keyboard. "What was the name again?"

"Ramsay, Daniel."

He made a few false starts. "I'm not good with computers." His nervous laugh was annoying. Bella stepped closer into his personal space.

"Found it. Yes." He read through the information on Daniel's ER stay.

"You were the doctor on duty that day," Bella said.

"Uh, yes. Yes, I signed in that morning." He kept his eyes on the computer and didn't turn to face her.

"What did you do when you got the call from the panic button?"

This time, his laugh was genuine as he wheeled around in his chair to face her. "The panic button? Surely, you're not serious. That thing hasn't worked since the 1990s."

Bella slapped him across the face. Hard. He reflexively reached up to touch his cheek that must have stung. He panicked.

"Looking for a panic button of your own, Arnie?" she hissed before she slapped him again. She put her hands around his neck and squeezed.

"This is what it feels like, Arnie. Your patient can't breathe. He's scared. He's helpless. He's waiting for his doctor who never comes."

"Help," he gasped as Bella pressed her fingers deeper into his carotid arteries. He flapped his arms in distress.

Bella flung him to the floor, where she kicked him in the groin. As he rolled around in pain, she repeatedly kicked him in the ribs. She rolled him over and stood on him and ground her five-inch narrow heels into his lower back and kidneys. He screamed in pain and released his bladder. She straddled him and yanked his head back by his hair while he lay in a pool of urine.

"You would've let Daniel die. My Daniel. He's mine. He's not yours to let slip away." Her voice had gone from a deadly hiss to an eerie shriek. She banged his head on the one-hundred-year-old tile floor. Once. Twice. Three times. His broken nose bled. His eyes were blinded by blood and sweat. The only sound he made was a gurgle.

She kicked his broken eyeglasses across the room, grabbed a computer cable, and knotted it. She looped it over his head and positioned herself so she could pull on it until he choked. She taunted him by pulling and releasing the cable.

"You bastard. You bastard. You bastard," she shouted. "I'm not going to let you die easily. Just remember who has the reins." She jerked on the cable and turned him over. She took off her shoes and was just about to stab him in the eye with a stiletto when she was grabbed from behind.

"Let me go." She struggled. "How can you even see me?" She'd become invisible during her rage.

"Bella. Bella, it's me," said the man softly and

authoritatively. "It's me, Bella. I've got you."

She turned to see her partner, who lived at Commonwealth Psych. He was helping her relocate the ghosts at Commonwealth who would need homes when the case was won and the hospital was condemned and closed. She tried to wrest herself from his grip and kicked the doctor one last time.

"Bella, stop. This quack is going to get what's coming to him. Don't ruin what you've started. Come on, step back."

She let him pull her away from the man who was silently lying on the floor.

"Is he dead?"

"Doubt it. Just beat up. Broken nose. Broken ribs. His pride, if he had any, is hurt."

Big pulled her to him and let her cry. "He could've let Daniel die. Daniel. My Daniel," she sobbed into his chest. She beat her fists against him until she exhausted herself and fell into his arms.

He stroked her hair. "Daniel's alive, Bella. He didn't die. He's still your Daniel," he whispered.

"You saved Daniel. LouLou told me about his heart attack during her deposition. She said you saved Daniel's life."

Big hugged her tightly. "I don't think it was a heart attack. It happened when he discovered LouLou was his child with you. He was highly emotional. I'm almost certain it was panic. Daniel was fragile. Any news, especially news about you, would have triggered a strong emotional response. I treated it like a heart attack to be safe. At worst, it may have been angina. LouLou didn't know anything. She just did what I told her. She may have thought it was a heart attack because of what I did, but I believe it was panic. He must have been given a sedative and immediately transferred to a private hospital. LouLou too."

Bella cried with relief. "You really don't think it was his heart?"

"No. I'm not a doctor, but I saw what happened first hand. The good thing was that it got both Dan and LouLou out of here and into private facilities where they were well-treated."

Panic. Not heart. Big wouldn't lie to her.

He held her in his thick arms against his chest for a long time. Finally, a chortle rose from his chest. "Bella," he tipped her chin up to make her look at him, "What's his story going to be? He got beat up by an invisible girl?"

A smile slowly came to her mouth. "You're right. He may become a patient."

"Or at least another ghost story for Commonwealth Psych," he said as he kissed the top of her head.

CHAPTER

TWENTY-SIX

The office was too quiet. No one from the AG's office had filed any motions.

A private graveside funeral service had been held for the not-so-Honorable Judge Paul Whiting in a public cemetery. Rumors circulated that only Anna, her husband, and John had attended. A Navy chaplain had conducted the service due to the unavailability of every Catholic priest in Richmond.

Margaret Whiting had been arrested, charged with first degree murder, and released on $250,000 bond. She retreated to a monastery run by an order of nuns at an undisclosed location within the state.

Bella and Mark continued the discovery phase of the case.

To reassure herself that every detail was on track, Bella suggested Mark call a short status meeting in the conference room. Opal took notes on a laptop while Mark ran the meeting.

"Let's get a sense of where we are. We're four

weeks away from trial." Mark looked at his team of two.

"Depositions?" Mark said. "Where are we with patient depositions?"

"All former patients on my list completed," Bella said.

"All former patients except one for me," Mark reported. "I'm meeting him at a hotel in Henrico County. His attorney said he's too ill to come to the office."

Daniel. Daniel was Mark's remaining patient. Nina Lombardi, Daniel's attorney, wasn't going to let some civil rights case derail Daniel's health. She'd make it as easy as possible for Daniel to comply with the subpoena. Good.

"Other former patients?" Mark asked Opal.

"All accounted for, including those who've died. The public notices for the two who remain unavailable have expired."

"Larry Yarbrough," said Bella quietly, referring to the man who'd been convicted of killing Evan Cooper. She was subtly reminding them he'd been a patient first and a killer second.

Mark nodded in acknowledgement. "Dr. Constantine continues to update me. He'll let me know as soon as Yarbrough is healthy and lucid enough to speak with some clarity. That might be on very short notice. Maybe a same-day trip. So, we have two remaining patient depositions."

Mark moved on. "Former hospital staff. Where are we on those?"

"Depositions from former doctors are scheduled for this week," Opal said.

Bella reported that she had completed deposing the former nursing staff, reviewed their employee records, and examined documents they'd provided.

"Current staff. What's up with them, Opal?"

"Some of them are fighting the subpoena. I have a list of them and their scheduled dates. They need responses," Opal said.

"I'll handle that this afternoon." Mark stretched his head and neck. "We're good on patients and staff. That leaves consultants. Opal, how's that going?"

Opal had been thorough. She'd itemized every piece of evidence.

"Expert witnesses. Drafts of expert witness testimony that the state failed to protect Evan Cooper from a violent Larry Yarbrough, who still had bath salts pumping through his body, are on your desk. Civil rights documents. I have transcripts of all the Human Rights Watch group meetings, including closed sessions. I have a tally of abuses that were reported and ignored. Also, there's a list of all the civil rights violations reported by the hospital to the state. I'm finalizing the chronology of federal guidelines to correct abuses starting in 1999. None of them have been followed."

"1999? Opal, that's almost twenty years the state has known about these violations," Bella noted.

Opal shrugged. "That's according to two documents."

Marked plowed on. "Motions?"

"The Motion for Summary Judgment is done except to fill in the blanks," Bella said quietly.

Mark smiled at Bella. Of course, it was done. It

had been done before Mark took the case.

"What's a Summary Judgment?" Opal seemed interested.

"It's a Fuck Off move to the AG's office," Mark explained. "It means we advise Judge King that everything she needs to know about the case is in our motion with its attachments. Every crime has several parts called elements. The plaintiff—that's us representing Evan Cooper—has to prove that every element of the crime was committed by the defendant—the Commonwealth represented by the AG's office—and is supported by admissible evidence.

"We say every single element of the crime was committed by the defendant and we have proof of that. The defense can't deny or refute our statements without committing perjury—lying to the court. No one in the AG's office is going to lie to Judge King. They'll be disbarred. We ask her to rule in favor of Evan Cooper's family now and save the state from a long expensive trial."

"What does the defense say?" Opal asked.

Mark smiled at his protégé. "They oppose our motion. First, they tell Judge King not all the elements of the crime have been committed. Second, they try to discredit our evidence for every element. In this case, they'll submit some convoluted reason because there aren't any actual reasons. If they convince Judge King even one of the elements doesn't have admissible evidence, she has no choice but to deny our motion and proceed to trial."

"That's not going to happen," Bella jumped in.

"Every element has been committed and we have double- and triple-checked the evidence for accuracy. The AG's office has nothing but BS. Judge King will see that and say let's not waste money for a trial that's going to end with the same result. She'll rule in favor of Evan Cooper's family."

"Awesome," Opal said. "I didn't know lawyers could be so cool."

Mark smiled again. "The judge has to be cool too. Judge King is a very smart woman and an excellent judge. She hates wasting time. She fines lawyers who are late. She denies postponements unless there's a colossal emergency as the reason for the request. She's not going to preside over a six-week trial to come up with the same verdict. We'll win on our Motion for Summary Judgment."

Opal's eyes darted between Bella and Mark. She looked stoked.

"Don't get too excited," Mark cautioned. "This is a once-in-a-lifetime case. It's not always so cool, but at least we're the good guys here."

Mark turned to Bella. "Did the AG's office follow through with the Notice of Appeal of Jurisdiction?"

"No," Bella said. "They never filed. They either forgot or considered it moot given the uproar when Judge Whiting was outed and then killed."

Mark nodded. "We win the case."

"What do we win?" Opal caught on quickly.

"Damages. It sounds odd, but the court will award what's called damages. It's almost always money. Sometimes there's a particular request granted. In this case, we've asked for both.

"When Judge King grants our Motion for Summary Judgment, she determines how Evan Cooper's family will be compensated for his death caused by the state. We've asked for twenty million dollars plus the closing of Commonwealth Psychiatric Hospital."

Bella turned to Opal. "Closing the hospital will insure that nothing like this will ever happen again in a state forensic hospital."

This was what Bella cared about. She could have accessed that amount of money and transferred it to the Cooper's bank account without going to trial. Unlike Opal, she had no qualms about stealing money. Bella wasn't a hacker, but she'd taught herself enough about accessing off-shore bank accounts of people she'd put in jail during her life as a securities lawyer to move money around. She knew white collar criminals who wouldn't notice that ten or twenty million dollars was missing.

"What about the patients? What happens to them?" Opal asked, brimming with interest.

Bella told her Mark had commissioned a private consulting firm to draft a plan to transfer patients from Commonwealth Psychiatric to appropriate facilities throughout the state.

"It's straightforward. Juvenile and geriatric patients can be moved to age-appropriate facilities. Drug detox patients go to rehab. Competency patients are either released for trial or moved to a treatment facility. A few patients will go to jail. One or two patients will need to be assessed for specific plans." Mark nodded. "That's a strong case to close the hospital. Patients can be transferred to more appropriate facilities and the state saves money in annual operating costs. The state also looks strong for righting such a grievous wrong."

"You're right," Opal announced. "We are the good guys."

"Good job, Opal. You've been great. Don't slack off now," Mark said. "The end is in sight."

CHAPTER
TWENTY-SEVEN

"I'm off to Henrico County for a deposition," Mark said.

Bella knew it was Daniel's. She'd been checking Mark's calendar daily. Because of Daniel's psychiatric history and unease in courtrooms, he'd be deposed in a hotel conference room near his home. He wouldn't even go to a law office. He wouldn't have to go far. His tiger attorney Nina Lombardi would accompany him. Good. Daniel had someone who was more than competent looking out for his interests.

Bella had arranged her schedule to be open during Daniel's deposition. She planned to be a ghost in the corner. She needed intense concentration to prevent Daniel from sensing her presence. She arrived early and quieted herself.

Daniel, wearing a navy blue suit, white oxford shirt, and no tie, looked thin but not gaunt when he entered the conference room with Nina. His face and hands showed he spent regular time in the sun. Good. He was keeping his routine of walking Ivan and running.

Mark was professional and reassuring. He shook Daniel's hand, offered him water or other drinks, and sat so Daniel would be able to look outside over a manmade lake.

"We'll stipulate to the prelims," Nina said. "Name, address, no alcohol or mind-altering substance this morning, regular meds, here voluntarily, dates of hospitalization. My client has limited endurance, so cut to the chase."

Mark acknowledged Nina, but still took time to relax Daniel.

"Mr. Ramsay, the topic today is exclusively your experience being a patient at Commonwealth Psychiatric Hospital. I'm not asking anything about your medical condition or criminal charges. I want your truthful answers about what your hospital stay was like. Understood?"

"Yes," Daniel said. No doubt Nina had coached him to answer in monosyllables unless asked to elaborate.

Bella's heart was breaking. Daniel looked so frail. So old. So witless. She couldn't find much of the spark of her Daniel except the rich sound of his voice and his unfailing good manners.

"Mr. Ramsay, did you feel safe at Commonwealth Psychiatric during your first inpatient admission?"

"I didn't feel anything for almost two years. I was in a catatonic state. I was sometimes aware people were in my hospital room."

"When you became aware of your surroundings, did you feel safe?"

"Yes."

"Were you afraid of other patients?"

"No."

"Afraid of the staff?"

"No."

"Do you recall the name of your doctor?"

"Dr. Harvey Chernoff."

"Was he on staff at Commonwealth Psychiatric?"

"No. He was a private physician who specialized in my condition. My brother hired him. Dr. Chernoff came to the hospital."

"Do you recall what he did differently from the doctors at Commonwealth Psych?"

Nina rested her hand on Daniel's arm. "Don't answer that," Nina said. "Rephrase or move on."

"What did Dr. Chernoff do when he visited you at the hospital?" Mark was as specific as Nina would allow.

"He put me in a lot of machines for tests. He gave me medication."

"Did he personally give you medication?" Bella was interested in the answer to this. Chernoff probably knew the likelihood of Daniel getting the prescribed medication from the hospital staff was low.

"Yes. He came every day with pills. He told me not to take anything else but his pills."

"After you'd been treated by Dr. Chernoff and felt better, did you interact with other people?"

"Yes."

"Who?"

"Other patients. I went to the day room every day."

"Do you recall anything unusual that happened with other patients?"

"Objection. Define unusual," Nina barked.

"Do you have a vivid memory from that time?"

"No."

"Do you remember being discharged from Commonwealth Psychiatric?"

"No."

"Do you remember being in Richmond Memorial Hospital after your stay at Commonwealth?"

"Yes."

"What happened there?"

"I saw Dr. Chernoff, got better, and went home. I mean, I went to my mother's house."

"Mr. Ramsay, would you like to take a break?"

Bella's heart broke off a little more when Daniel looked to Nina like a child would search a teacher's face for the correct answer.

"Dan, do you want to use the men's room?" Nina said.

"Yes."

"We'll take a break," Nina said decisively and stood.

***

Bella had to remain impassive. If she emoted even a bit, Daniel would sense her. She watched the two men who were in her life now. Mark, who was handsome and smart enough and sexy, and Daniel, who had once been three times more handsome, smart, and sexy but was now a shell of himself. Her greatest desire at that moment was not to take Daniel away with her, but to give him a double chocolate milkshake. If only he could gain weight and muscle tone, he'd be more like the Daniel she remembered. He had to be well enough to pass with her to eternity.

Daniel and Nina returned. Mark continued his easy questioning without being condescending.

"Mr. Ramsay, you were hospitalized a second time at Commonwealth Psychiatric. Did you feel safe then?"

"At first, all I felt was loneliness. I wanted to be with my daughter."

"After you began treatment, did you become aware of people other than your daughter?"

"Yes."

"You attended group therapy sessions?"

"Yes."

"You went to the day room?"

"Yes."

"Did you feel safe? In your group sessions and the day room?"

"Not consciously."

Nina again. "Get to the point, counselor."

"Mr. Ramsay, did you feel unsafe at any time during your second stay at Commonwealth Psychiatric Hospital?"

"No," Daniel responded.

"Did you wear something to identify you as a patient serving a NGRI sentence?"

"Rephrase," Nina said.

"Was your hospital wristband a different color from anyone else's?"

"No."

"Did you live on a ward with men and women or just men?

"Both."

"Do you remember patients who were on high on drugs when they came in?"

"Yes, they were always loud." Daniel shook his head as if he could still hear them shouting and laughing and fighting.

"Were they moved so they wouldn't be so loud around other patients?"

"No. They kept me awake at night."

"Did you tell any of the staff about the noise?"

"One time in group, I said I hadn't slept because of too much noise. It sounded like two men who were on drugs were fighting on my ward."

"Did things change after you mentioned that?"

"No. Loud guys came until I left."

"Did you spend time with any other patients outside of treatment?"

"No. When I went to the day room, I liked to look outside. There was a chair by the window I liked. The members of my group went back to their rooms after our sessions."

"Why was that?"

Nina's hand shot out to signal Daniel to remain silent. "Nice try, rephrase."

"Mr. Ramsay, am I correct in saying you interacted with the patients in your group during sessions and you didn't talk to anyone in the day room?"

"Yes. I always said hello to Big in the day room, but we didn't have conversations."

"Do you know Big's real name?"

"No. I remember he was there during my first stay and then the second. He was always in the day room. He was always polite to me."

"Where did you eat?"

"In my room."

"Do you recall seeing this man during either stay?" Mark showed him a photograph of Evan Cooper.

"No."

"What about this man?" Mark showed him a photograph of Larry Yarbrough.

"No."

"Mr. Ramsay, were you ever sick during either of your stays?"

"Yes."

"What happened?"

Bella leaned in. She dreaded hearing about his near-fatal heart attack.

"I cut my finger on a metal folding chair. An aide gave me a band-aid."

"Thank you, Mr. Ramsay. This concludes the deposition." Mark added all the required information for the record.

Silent tears streamed down Bella's face

CHAPTER
TWENTY-EIGHT

Two straight days of rain. Drop after drop after drop of rain matched Bella's mood. She'd underestimated her endeavor. Mark relied on her. She felt drained. She'd planned to use him as her mouthpiece to get justice for Daniel, LouLou, and any other soul who'd endured the hell that was Commonwealth Psychiatric Hospital. He was that, but not much else. She'd been the one to find Opal. Without Opal, they'd never be racing to the finish line.

She'd devoted more time to Mark than she'd planned. At first, she needed to lure him into taking the case and staying the course. She liked him. He was a good lover. Bottom line, he was lazy.

Without her prodding, he'd still be living in an unfurnished house, believing he was part of the old boys club, and getting by on charm and his family name. He enjoyed playing the non-conformist in the small, suffocating circle of Richmond society. He actually thought he was an outsider until she showed him what that really felt like. He'd been hurt before he became angry. Anger she could use. Bella didn't want to tend his hurt.

She wondered what kind of future he envisioned for himself. He knew the dating circle in Richmond was downright incestuous, yet he hadn't made a move to find someone somewhere else. Granted, girls who hung out at marina bars on the Chesapeake Bay weren't likely to be ideal, but surely there were women sailors. Women who were successful enough to own boats, captain boats, race boats. Invigorating women who were adventurous enough to sail solo. Fun women.

Mark was thirty-five and lived as though he was seventy-five without children and grandchildren to enjoy. Maybe he should go on that TV show where eligible bachelors choose a fiancée from twenty-five beauty contestants. She smiled at the thought of that being her best advice for him. She couldn't fix him. She didn't want to.

After seeing Daniel at the deposition, she chided herself for even considering Mark to having anything close to Daniel's character and capacity to love. Even broken, Daniel forced himself to be dressed, shaved, and well-mannered. He was thoughtful and eager to contribute what he could to the case. He was dependent on his lawyer, but who else could he trust given what the medical system had done to him? Bella was thrilled he had a smart cookie like Nina to protect him.

Bella was weary. Her heart had been shattered into so many pieces during her life, she was certain parts of it were dust. She'd healed as much as she could. She had to stay whole for Daniel. For the two of them. For eternity.

She replayed their lovemaking in her mind. They'd once tried to count all the places where they'd had sex and ended up losing count in a fit of laughter. They'd made such joyous love. They'd been happy.

At UVA, Daniel read the bad, but increasingly better, poems he wrote for her before bed. He had such a good ear for music that he could listen outside her practice room and identify infinitesimal nuances she'd tried and either added and discarded. The most endearing thing he did was to document their lives in scrapbooks. He kept everything: concert ticket stubs, reviews of her piano recitals, and odd memorable pieces from paper napkins to beer logo coasters.

Their favorite place to be together was the beach, especially at her parents' house in St. John, where they swam and snorkeled in crystalline turquoise waters. They ate tree-fresh coconut, papaya, and mango, made sun tea and ginger beer, and slept in a hammock under the stars. They'd been young, naive enough, and deliriously happy.

Even when Mørk first appeared, it didn't seem so bad. They learned together how to combat it. At the first hint of Mørk, Daniel made sure to run every day, eat healthy foods on a strict timetable, and abstain from alcohol. He slept eight hours every night. Just by imposing a schedule, Mørk could be diminished. She never left Daniel during those episodes. She'd miss class and go to his with him. She learned far more about macroeconomics than she ever wanted, but she was there. With Daniel. Beating back what would become debilitating depression.

Bella skipped work during those two rainy days. On the second afternoon, she got an unexpected phone call. LouLou wanted to see her.

CHAPTER
TWENTY-NINE

LouLou was waiting by the open industrial door to her loft when Bella got off the elevator. "Thank you for inviting me, LouLou."

LouLou said nothing. She closed and bolted the door. Bella walked in and surveyed the enormous undivided loft with minimal furniture. An ebony concert grand piano, a platform bed with built-in nightstands and lights, and a designer sectional sofa in ombré stripes of green velvet were the only pieces.

"You have a wonderful home. Lots of natural light. It's perfect." Especially for a schizophrenic who needed to keep her mood stable and in the worst case, avoid hurting herself by minimizing the amount of sharp edges and breakable *objets d'art*.

LouLou headed toward the galley kitchen and refilled her water glass. Bella noticed LouLou's skinny jeans hung loosely on her. Her baby blue cashmere cardigan could have wrapped around her twice. She wore no makeup. Diamond stud earrings. She was barefoot. She looked worse than when Bella had taken her deposition.

LouLou took the water with big ice chunks in a crystal glass and skittered to the sofa, tucked her feet underneath her, and pulled her sweater tighter.

Bella sat on the section of the sofa facing LouLou.

"Are you unwell? Are you cold?" Bella asked.

LouLou silently shook her head. This was going to be tedious if LouLou didn't speak up about what she wanted. Bella knew she hadn't been summoned for a friendly chat.

She tried again. "Have you eaten?"

"Yes," she said. Bella doubted it meant more than a few bites of something. Wasn't someone overseeing her food intake? LouLou's regimen wasn't her concern so she accepted LouLou's answer.

"I didn't know what to get you, so I brought a notebook. A lovely blue suede cover with blank pages. We can never have too many places to write." She smiled and placed the book tied with a white satin ribbon on the cushion next to LouLou.

"I never wanted you here," LouLou announced. "I thought you and Dan would contaminate my space, but I have no choice. Only five people in the world know where I live. Please don't tell anyone, especially Dan."

"No, I won't," Bella said. Who would she tell? Dan was forbidden to contact LouLou; she had a permanent restraining order against him. Bella had already accessed the apartment when LouLou wasn't around to get a sense of the floorplan and do some necessary tasks.

"I don't like what you did," LouLou blurted. "I'd never have known I was adopted if you hadn't given me a blind trust to be opened when I was thirty. I didn't need to know. I love my parents, not you and Dan. I'm glad I gave away the money."

Bella easily pretended she didn't know LouLou had given away the money, but she wasn't going to let LouLou create a fantasy about how she learned of her adoption.

"LouLou, that's not true. My understanding is that the lieutenant governor investigated irregularities at Petersburg when an aide accessed confidential DNA databases and told you Daniel was your father. As to the money, it was yours to do with whatever you please. It was a gift. You're not accountable to me."

LouLou paused, but resumed her almost childish outrage.

"You broke your promise. You and my parents had an agreement not to tell me I was adopted. Setting up that trust broke that promise. In your note, you said you set it up when I was born. You lied to them before I was born. You never intended to keep your promise."

Anger rose within Bella, but she had to tamp it down. No one dared question her integrity when she lived as a human. She'd have ruined anyone who had. Her ghostly life was much less laudable. She'd lied, stolen, and murdered when she had to. No laws constrained her now. LouLou questioning her integrity when she was alive was unacceptable.

Bella was firm and direct with LouLou.

"I don't know what the Flemings told you, but I know the documents we signed. The documents expired—ceased to be legally binding—when you became an adult at eighteen. Yes, I provided funds to be given to you well after you became an adult. A dozen years afterward. Even to me at age twenty-two, the Flemings appeared to be old. Reports on their health indicated they shouldn't die before you became an adult, but their financial resources weren't vast. Your father was a civil servant. Your mother's family was wealthy, but not spectacularly so. Women need money of their own. I couldn't predict the future. I didn't know how much you'd earn or whether you'd marry someone who was financially well-off. I intended to make sure my daughter had a small financial cushion. *C'est tout.*"

LouLou sat upright. "What do you mean your reports on my parents? You investigated them?"

Bella made one of her most delightful, trilling laughs.

"LouLou, I'm not the ogre you seem to have imagined me to be." Bella moved closer to LouLou. "Even as a young student, I knew a child of mine with Daniel would be bright and special and deserve everything the world offered. I'd no intention of relying on adoption agency reports. I conducted independent private inquiries both in Washington, DC and Paris. There were candidates who were far wealthier, younger, and more prestigious than the Flemings, but the Flemings desperately wanted you. They thrived on all the things Daniel and I do—music, art, books—and they were loving people."

Bella stood directly in front of the sofa where LouLou sat with a scowl on her face.

"LouLou, make no mistake. I chose the Flemings. I rejected other couples I was pressured to accept. The Flemings were the best family for you. I knew it from my investigations and from meeting them. Whatever monetary concerns I had about them could be offset by a small blind trust. The reason you have them as parents was my decision, not theirs."

LouLou's small shoulders slumped. Apparently, it had never occurred to this dim, self-centered woman that the biological mother decided where her baby was placed. The Flemings hadn't selected her from a cabbage patch of adoptable infants. Again, Bella marveled that she and Daniel had produced such a naïf creature. Schizophrenia was the least of LouLou's problems.

LouLou didn't move or speak. Bella really had reached her limit of patience. She sat on the sofa away from LouLou and spoke softly.

"*Ma cher*, what's troubling you? What can I do to help?" Bella didn't want to spook LouLou. Quite frankly, she wouldn't know what to do if LouLou started to have an episode. She was out of her element. She at least had the telephone number of LouLou's psychiatrist in her phone from the day of the deposition.

"I'm in love with a ghost," LouLou whispered. "He left and I don't know how to get him back. It's been more than a year and I can't pull myself together. I do all the right things. I take my meds, give myself injections, and see my psychiatrist. I exercise, eat properly, get lots of rest. None of it matters. I'm so sad I can't stand it."

Ah. LouLou was certainly Daniel's daughter. She felt things deeply and irreversibly. "I'm sorry."

"I can't even talk to anyone about him. I never told my friends or family I had a man in my life." She looked at Bella with those unusual eyes. "Bella, how can I make him come back?"

Ah, Gregg. Bella had limits as to what she could say. After all, she'd been the one to take Gregg away.

"LouLou, what makes you think I can help?"

LouLou blinked at her with those abnormally large blue eyes as though the answer was obvious. "You're a ghost. You know how ghosts think. You said you'd be gone in two years and you have a plan. You're the only one who can help me."

Bella really didn't know how to respond. LouLou didn't seem to notice and her questions kept coming.

"Just tell me what it's like. How did you become a ghost? The aide at the hospital said you were a crazy criminal who killed yourself."

This she could easily handle.

"I'm not a criminal," Bella lied. Technically, her crimes were committed after she became a ghost. She'd been a law-abiding human. "Perhaps the aide meant I committed a sin. It doesn't matter.

"I never had a mental illness. I died of grief. I was thirty when my husband died suddenly of an aggressive cancer. Nine months later, three hundred seventy-two people who were my colleagues, clients, and friends were killed on 9/11 in the World Trade Center. I was at a meeting in midtown.

Otherwise, I would've been among then. No matter. I literally sat in my apartment getting phone call after phone call that people I was close to had died. I don't recall whether I turned off my phone or cell reception ceased. My heart couldn't hold anymore grief."

"Your husband? You married someone else? Not Dan?"

Bella nodded. "Yes. I met a fantastic man and we had a fabulous life together until his death. I didn't intend to become a nun because I couldn't be with Daniel."

"You had almost four hundred friends?" LouLou seemed incredulous.

This girl, her child, flitted from topic to topic. She couldn't focus. She seemed more damaged than Bella could handle, but she put aside her feelings long enough to answer.

"LouLou, I knew them from work, law school, and through my husband. Some were my closest friends. All of them died. Just evaporated in less than an hour. I couldn't grieve enough. I grieved too much. I hanged myself and it was over."

Bella willed herself not to cry. She sat still and waited. LouLou would eventually say what she wanted or needed.

"How did you know to come back? Did you come back for Dan?"

"And you," Bella responded. "I was in the ambulance with you after that accident at Christmas. I stayed until your uncle got to the hospital. I sensed you needed me."

"The accident was when Gregg left."

"I see." Having caused the accident that precipitated Gregg's departure, Bella remained silent. She could hardly kill another ghost, but she'd transported him to another spot on the globe to separate the couple. Payback. LouLou had sent Daniel back to Petersburg. If Bella couldn't have her lover, she made sure LouLou didn't have hers.

Also, with her father dead and Gregg gone, Bella hoped LouLou would accept Daniel into her life. She hadn't. She cost Daniel more time in Commonwealth Psych when he'd been so desperate to see LouLou. She'd filed charges that he was cyber-stalking her. Silly woman. Even with the loss of Gregg, LouLou didn't relent regarding Daniel.

"LouLou, ghosts return when they need to finish something. For me, I must close that hospital and be with Daniel. Did Gregg say why he came to you?"

She started to cry. "He said he'd always known I'd be the woman he loved. He was a musician—a composer. He spent thirteen years at Commonwealth Psych, composed all that time, and stored the music in his head. With me, it was recorded, published, and performed.

"It wasn't all about music. Gregg loved me. The barn owl tattoo. That was our symbol. He suggested drawing one because it was beautiful and monogamous just like you said. I thought you must know Gregg because you knew about the owl."

"LouLou, darling, I don't know him. Most people who grew up in Virginia have seen barn owls. Was he from here?"

"Norfolk," she whispered.

"Tidewater, then. I grew up in Virginia Beach.

We saw the same wildlife. I'm sure he knew about egrets and cardinals and thrashers. None of that means I could pick him out in a crowd."

LouLou seemed to believe her. She hugged her sweater tighter. "Gregg loved me. He came back as a ghost for me, but he left without me. I want him back. Tell me what to do, Bella. Please."

CHAPTER THIRTY

LouLou sounded dangerously distressed, but the most interesting thing to Bella was that Gregg had a connection to Commonwealth Psych. "Gregg was at Petersburg?"

LouLou nodded. "He wasn't a psych patient, though. He was mentally healthy."

This sounded odd, but Bella let LouLou continue. She spoke in fits and starts so Bella had no intention of interrupting her.

"Things must have been very different then," LouLou said. "He was picked up as an undesirable in the 1960s and released one night years later. He didn't know what a discharge plan was when I asked him. He said the night nurse woke him and told him to leave, unlocked the door, and let him walk out at midnight. He was disoriented and fell into a creek and drowned."

"That's horrifying. I'm sorry for him." Bella wondered if it was true. There was more to the story if he had unfinished business and became a ghost.

"He came back to be with me and to compose as

he was meant to do. Do you think his reasons were accomplished? Is he at peace, or can he come back?"

Of course, he could come back. He hadn't finished his mission. Bella had interrupted it.

"He wasn't good at being a ghost. He was invisible except to me, a Sensitive, and Dan." Tears streaked LouLou's cheeks.

"Daniel is a Sensitive," Bella said decisively.

"That explains it. Gregg couldn't do any of the things you do. You're visible to everyone. You shake hands with people. Everyone can hear you. How do you do it?"

"Ghosts are people in another form. We're all different. I was in a hole of grief for probably the first five years of being a ghost. When I realized I was a ghost, I experimented until I could do things. I made a lot of mistakes. I'm entirely self-taught so I don't know what others do. I didn't have control of myself for a long time. Even now, it takes great concentration to be visible or invisible to everyone."

Bella was going to have to pry everything out of LouLou. "What did Gregg say about his abilities?"

"He said he didn't know where he went when he wasn't with me or at the record store where he spent most of his time. He was nervous about traveling to places he'd never been. He and Skylar, the friend who is a Sensitive, experimented with short car trips and then longer ones. He took a bus trip once. He never went from one place to another by just concentrating.

"He said he didn't know how long he had with me. When it was time to go, he said he couldn't help himself and left. I was surprised when you sounded so confident that you'd be here months, if not years. How do you know?"

"That's my mission. That's how long it takes. I can't tell you more than that. I don't know."

LouLou started to cry again. "Bella, tell me everything you know about ghosts. Any detail. Where do you go when you're alone? How do you have so many clothes? What do you do about eating in public? Do you know other ghosts?"

These were all easy questions and completely irrelevant to coaxing Gregg back.

"Darling, it really comes down to lying and stealing. I get clothes by invisibly going to stores when they're closed, trying things on, and wearing them when I leave. Sometimes, I put things back if it was a one occasion dress.

"Ghosts eat like anorexics. I'm vigilant about food. I've developed hundreds of excuses—I just ate, I'll get something to go, I'm fasting today—anything to deflect attention from what I'm not eating. In situations where it would be rude not to eat, I move food around on my plate, slip it into my napkin, and discard it. I've found if I walk around with an apple and a bottle of water, the issue of whether I'm eating never occurs to most people.

"I can only tell you my experience. I live among Sensitives and other ghosts. We meet in places ghosts seem to enjoy. London, for example. When I don't want to socialize, I disappear. I go nowhere. It's not a place. It's just blank.

"You'd call it dozing. I keep an eye on my mission and anything that affects it, but otherwise, I just wait.

"The main point about ghosts is that we're people in another form. We don't gain any special powers by dying. I can't practice witchcraft or foresee the future or reverse time. I can't read people's thoughts any better than I could when I was human. I can't will things to happen. All I can do is what I used to do although now that I'm invisible, I can do it secretly."

"Like what?"

"Obviously, I walk through walls. That's how I got here. I didn't think you'd want to explain who I was to your neighbors should they ask."

"Gregg could do that. What else?"

"Let me think." She couldn't tell her that she'd just popped into LouLou's loft two years ago and left her a note. She couldn't tell her about the case. Something benign.

"For example, if I needed a hat that I knew was in a trunk in someone's attic, I couldn't just will the hat to come to me. I'd have to go into the house without making a sound if someone was home and into the attic. I'd hunt around until I found the trunk and then I'd look through everything until I found the hat. Then I'd leave. The worst that could happen is someone might see a hat walking itself down the stairs. They'd never be able to see or feel me so they'd just think the wind blew it."

LouLou didn't respond. Maybe she was thinking. Or spacing out. Bella had no idea. She'd never have survived motherhood. It was too stressful.

"Gregg wouldn't lie or steal," LouLou finally said.

"Do you know that for certain?"

She nodded. "When he was here, if he needed something, like to rent an oboe for a month, he had Skylar rent it for him. He always insisted I buy two movie tickets even if no one would see him. He never lied to me or Skylar."

Admirable, but not helpful to a prolonged life as a ghost.

"That's my experience. Perhaps other ghosts use different techniques."

"Gregg didn't seem to get any better at being a ghost. He looked online, but all he could find was information about ghost sightings. Nothing about ghost behavior."

"Do you mind if I stand and walk around?" Bella needed something to do so she could think.

LouLou shrugged, but cautioned her. "Don't even think about touching the piano."

Bella walked to one of the enormous windows and looked over the river. She couldn't help LouLou. She had no idea where Gregg was now. He could still be in Phuket, unwilling or unable to travel back to LouLou. He wasn't practiced at space travel. He could take regular transportation if he'd become street smart in order to get money and tickets. She'd tell LouLou generalities and let her take it from there.

CHAPTER
THIRTY-ONE

Bella walked back to the sofa and sat. "LouLou, ghosts are drawn to places we've been or somewhere that was significant. We follow people to whom we have an attachment. You're obviously Gregg's person, so he'd probably follow you. He died on the grounds of the hospital in Petersburg, is that right?"

"I think so. He said he was looking for a road. I don't know where the creek was."

Bella wanted to scream. LouLou was hopeless. Schizophrenia or not, LouLou seemed to have no reasoning ability or inquisitive nature. She could've Googled Commonwealth Psych to look at a map and hadn't done it. She'd just sat. Waiting.

"That's something to research. Google the hospital. Look for a creek on or near the grounds of the hospital. Look at the Petersburg newspapers. There was probably a morning and evening edition back then. There might have been a newspaper

186

article about a man drowning around the time he died."

"Okay." LouLou made no move to write down the suggestions.

"Your loft is important to you and Gregg. Anywhere else?"

"Vinyl, the record store Skylar owns. Gregg went there every day. The art house theatre on Cary Street. We went there a lot."

"You went other places, but they weren't significant, right?"

"I don't know." More tears.

"LouLou, I'm trying to help, but you have to do the work. I can only do so much."

LouLou looked at her with something close to contempt. Bella ignored it and made a sincere suggestion.

"Take the notebook I just gave you and write that you should do a Google search on information about Gregg's death. There might be clues if there's a newspaper article. Then write down the places you and Gregg went regularly or once if it was significant enough. I'd start with the Exit Number on I-95, where he left."

The notebook came with a pen. LouLou picked it up and looked at the blank pages. She was overcome and started to sob. Between heaving sobs, LouLou asked for her tote bag. Bella found a red leather tote near the piano and handed it to her. LouLou dug around for a slick silver pill case and slipped a blue pill under her tongue. She held out her glass for a refill of water. Bella freshened her glass with ice and chilled water.

After about ten minutes, LouLou stopped crying and looked at Bella with animosity. "What then? What if I make a list of all the places that were important. Then what? Am I supposed to just camp out there until he shows up? I've been sitting in this loft every day since he left and he hasn't shown up here."

Good. LouLou had some life in her. There was hope.

"Then I'd say you can cross this off your list," she said reasonably. "Skylar will tell you if he appears at Vinyl. So that crosses two off the list. You don't have to do it this minute. Think about a place and decide if it's likely that Gregg would expect you to be there."

LouLou seemed relieved at the thought of two places that could be crossed off her list.

"What if I'm not home when Gregg comes?"

Bella held her temper. "LouLou, if Gregg has come back from the dead for you, he's not going to give up if you happen to be out for a walk when he returns. He'll wait."

LouLou brightened at that thought and then plunged into the darkness around her.

"Bella, what if I killed myself? I wouldn't die of natural causes and maybe I could find Gregg in the ghost world."

"There is no ghost world. There are places that are important to individual ghosts. There are lots of ghosts in London, but it's not a place where all ghosts go. Has Gregg ever been to London?"

LouLou shook her head.

"Then there's absolutely no reason to think he'd

be there. You must concentrate on what's important to Gregg. From what you've told me, that's you and his compositions."

"I don't want to live without him. My entire life centers on taking enough meds to keep me from hurting other people. That's not a reason to live."

"It's a reason to give Gregg time to return. If his mission isn't finished and you don't believe it is, then he'll return if he can find his way. It's hard. You said yourself Gregg isn't very good at being a ghost. Maybe he'll find a mentor who'll help him."

That quieted LouLou for a while. After what seemed like hours to Bella, LouLou asked the question she really wanted answered.

"How could Gregg have been a ghost? He died by drowning. Isn't that a natural cause?"

Bella was very close to losing her temper.

"Gregg was killed. That hospital is corrupt. He was most likely drugged and sent out a secret exit that was nowhere near a road. If they needed the bed or were angry with him or just didn't like him, they would have gotten rid of him."

"Gregg said they thought he was gay," LouLou sniffled.

"Perhaps that was the reason. Some homophobic staff wanted him out of there. I don't know why, but I'm certain his drowning wasn't an accident."

LouLou seemed to grasp the concept. She sat silently, staring at nothing for a while.

Bella was finished. She'd told LouLou what she could. She wasn't going to sit and watch LouLou stare into space or think or whatever it was she was doing.

"I'm going to leave. Do you want someone to be with you? Skylar, maybe? He might help you with the list. Or maybe you should rest. Don't tire yourself. An episode is absolutely the last thing that will bring Gregg back."

"Is it?"

"I don't know why I said that. It seems logical."

"No, don't call anyone. I'll be fine by myself."

"I hope I've helped. If I think of anything else, how should I reach you?"

"Leave a message for me at Vinyl. Skylar will get it to me."

Bella took one last look at the child who was hers with Daniel. She couldn't comprehend the three of them together. She and Dan were a pair. Bella and Daniel. She didn't think there ever would have been a place for LouLou. The Flemings had loved her when she couldn't.

"Good-bye, LouLou."

CHAPTER

THIRTY-TWO

Conversations in multiple languages and several dialects of English she didn't understand buzzed as Bella stood at the top of the steps to the basement of Commonwealth Psychiatric Hospital. She had wanted to meet the twenty-six resident ghosts in the day room, but had been persuaded the basement would be more comfortable for everyone. The day room with its electricity, plumbing, and twenty-first century furniture would frighten some of the oldest residents.

She cautiously descended. She had to persuade the residents she was honest and had their best interests in mind. They'd been lied to far too long.

Her sheer beauty stopped every conversation. Bella was used to that, but not in front of other ghosts. She walked confidently to the front of the room and winked at her colleague. He introduced her. By doing so, he vouched for her seriousness and purpose for some. For others, she'd have to earn their trust.

"Good evening," she said just before midnight. "My name is Bella, and I have a plan to give us all rest and peace. Some of you may find peace tonight just in the news I bring. For the rest, we'll plan your path.

"The time is the twenty-first century. We're in Petersburg, Virginia in one of the fifty states of the United States of America. Wars are over. The war between the states ended in 1864 when Confederate Army General Robert E. Lee surrendered to United State Army General Ulysses S. Grant. Every one of every race, religion, and gender is free. Slavery is illegal."

"Impossible," coughed one young soldier.

"Yet, it's true." She paused as two ghosts slipped away.

"The President of the United States is a black man who was educated at Harvard University. Members of Congress are men and women of black, white, Hispanic, and Asian descent. The Supreme Court is composed of black, white, and Hispanic men and women.

"The First World War ended in 1918 with a victory for the Allies, including the United States. The Second World War ended in 1945 with a victory for the Allies, including the United States. The Korean War is over although the United States, along with other countries, maintains a presence in South Korea. The United States withdrew troops from Vietnam in 1974."

Three more ghosts departed. Twenty-one souls remained.

"Most of you know, this institution houses a brutal, inhumane regime. People are neglected, tortured, and killed in the guise of mental health treatment. That is going to stop. This hospital will be closed and I hope, taken down, brick by brick." Bella held up her hand. "I know this is the only home you've had for many years. Don't be frightened. My colleague and I are here to help you find peace and rest before the building is closed. You won't be harmed. You'll have a new home.

"We'll meet individually with you and create a plan. As you see, five of you have found peace just in the knowledge of the truths I've told. I'd like it to be as simple as that for all of you, but you each have a reason for remaining here and may need individual guidance.

"I speak English, French, and Italian. My colleague knows many dialects. We'll find a way to communicate. We'll start planning whenever you're ready. Thank you."

***

The hour before sunrise was precious. Bella saw blue in the night sky become more vivid before the reds and golds rose in the east. She sat outside alone, having worked through the night. Five more ghosts departed after learning that a certain plantation owner, a Confederate soldier, and Herr Hitler were dead.

Most of the ghosts wanted to know what had happened to specific people or wanted to be properly buried with their families. One army medic suffered from PTSD from the Vietnam War. He needed to know the bombs in his head were no longer coming for him. Three ghosts wanted to go home. Two women wanted to see their descendants.

The most heartbreaking ghost was a man who had been institutionalized since 1871 because he was homeless and illiterate. He didn't know what he wanted other than to be safe. He cried and asked if he could stay. Bella promised to help him find what he needed.

She couldn't rest until she'd helped them all.

Big moved to sit beside her. He put his arms around her and hugged her. "You set the perfect tone. They trust you too, now."

She rested her head on his chest.

"You're amazing. I know you're working around the clock on the lawsuit, but these souls needed to meet you. I'm glad you took the time to come."

Bella couldn't look at Big. She was crying. "They're all so frightened. They've never been able to trust anyone."

"Most of them trust me. They'll trust me more now that they've met my partner on the outside who is doing all the legal maneuvering. Nice touch to wear a suit and bring your briefcase with legal papers. You added credibility to what I've told them.

"Now that they know someone can provide answers and peace, they'll open up to me. They'll tell me what they need to get peace. Once I get their stories, you said your assistant Opal can research how to do that. The ones who are left mostly want to be with their families."

Bella's tears still fell.

"Families. I'm sure some of their families put them here to be rid of them," she spat.

"Maybe they never knew their families. Those military men probably have families all over the United States who never knew what happened to them. We just need to find the cemeteries with family plots, if nothing else."

"Opal can do that."

Big offered his enormous hand to help her stand. "Nice touch, counselor, throwing in a bit of Caribbean patois." He smiled.

Bella returned the smile. "I grew up on St. John in the United States Virgin Islands. Caribbean islanders speak a mix of many things."

She put her hand on his arm. "Thank you. You're doing all this by yourself."

"It's nothing. I've been here a long time. Watching. Listening."

CHAPTER
THIRTY-THREE

Bella and Mark were reviewing exhibits when Opal walked in with papers. "These were just served," she said.

Mark glanced at them and laughed. "Typical. Three thirty on a Friday afternoon with a response, including oral argument, due Monday morning." He looked pointedly at Bella.

"Why is that typical?" Opal asked. Bella was pleased with Opal's interest in the chess game lawyers played. Of course, nothing would ever be as heady for her as computer hacking.

Mark explained. "Big firms or large government offices like the AG's serve motions that require an immediate response on small firms Friday afternoons because they think it makes us work through the weekend."

"Wouldn't they have to work through the weekend too?" Opal asked.

"Probably not. They've been ready for a while,

but waited until Friday afternoon to notify us. Worst case, someone in their office has to work through the weekend, but not the most senior staff. They think I'm working alone with you and think they're gaining an advantage—overworking me so I'll make a mistake."

"That's not fair," Opal said.

Mark made his crinkly-eyed laugh. "Justice isn't fair. Nothing is, really." He stretched behind his desk. "This doesn't matter. It requires a two-sentence response and a quick oral argument."

"The motion is to postpone the trial," Bella guessed.

Mark nodded.

"How did you know that?" Opal asked. She seemed to be fascinated by the entire process.

"It's a tactic. We want to get to trial on time. They want to stall. It's not uncommon." Bella shrugged.

"Wow. Lawyers are way cooler than I thought," Opal said on her way out.

"You think she's going to take the LSAT?" Mark was half serious.

"No," Bella said. "She's smart, but she doesn't have the patience for law school. Of course, Virginia remains the only state where she can take the bar without attending law school if she studies under an experienced practitioner…"

"Did she go to college?"

"I've no idea, but we're not here to discuss Opal's career path. Let's finish. We're going away for the weekend."

Mark looked at her with his sweet blue eyes. "Do

I have to pack?"

"No, just a passport. You can get what you need there. Our flight is at six. File an answer and let's go."

***

Bella arranged for a small private jet. She didn't want to encounter airport security, flight attendants, and other passengers. Mark didn't seem surprised to be on a private flight and made no comment other than to ask where they were going. She told him it was a surprise.

When they landed in warm, breezy Bermuda that evening, Mark was thrilled. He hugged her to him. "I've never been. What a clever woman you are."

She laughed and led him to the motor scooter rental area.

"What are we doing here?" he asked. He eyed a long line of shiny red motor scooters, most of which had reserved signs on them.

"No one drives cars in Bermuda. They ride scooters. You can drive one, can't you?" She smiled that enticing Bella smile.

"I rode dirt bikes as a kid. I'll give it a try." He conferred with the attendant about scooters and how to operate one. Mark signed a release, donned a helmet, and took one for a test spin around the lot. He ended with a huge grin on his face. Bella found his boyish enthusiasm charming.

The attendant rented Mark a bike, cautioned him to drive on the left side of the road, and advised him to give way to traffic in the rotaries. He didn't say anything to Bella and only offered Mark one helmet. When Mark asked for a second, the attendant gave it to him with a knowing smile. Mark started the scooter, Bella sat behind him, and they flew around the island to their hotel—the venerable old Princess in Hamilton that had not yet succumbed to renovation.

"It's beautiful here," Mark said that evening as they sat in the courtyard with their feet on the stone bulkhead overlooking the harbor. "The pastel houses on the hill across from us are amazing. The motor bike. The harbor traffic. I want to sail, don't you?"

"If you insist, but you have a tee time tomorrow," she reminded him. She'd never told him how deadly dull she found sailing.

"Do you play golf?" he asked.

"No, but you do. There are excellent courses here you should try. I'm sure the pro will pair you with someone fun."

"What are you going to do?" He looked worried. She wondered if he thought she was meeting another lover while he was distracted.

"Shop. There are lovely shops here." She would look around and return after the stores closed if she needed anything. She'd purchased a white one-piece swimsuit with strategic cut-outs in the hotel shop and charged it to the room.

"Speaking of which," he turned to her and held her hand, "what about golf clothes? We didn't bring any luggage."

"I'm sure you can find something at the clubhouse to wear." She kissed him. "And clubs."

She kissed him again. "And golf balls." She kissed him a third time.

"We need to go to our room," he said.

CHAPTER

THIRTY-FOUR

Bella was delighted to encounter a ghost she'd known in human form in Paris while Mark played golf the next morning. Lena had died with her husband in a skiing accident due to deliberate equipment failure and was in this realm to oversee the upbringing of her twin daughters. Their paternal aunt, who was too stodgy for Lena's taste, had custody. Bella and Lena spent the afternoon at the pool wearing large sunhats and gossiping.

"Do the girls live in Bermuda?" Bella asked.

"London, but the family vacations in Bermuda. It's really a lovely place to be a ghost. There are several of us scattered around the island. One is a delectable young man who died in a shipwreck in the seventeenth century. He's waiting for his True Love to find him. I suppose it's possible and I do look for her when I'm in London."

"Can't you take him to London?" Bella puzzled.

"He's afraid of airplanes. He doesn't know what

will happen to him. I've told him I fly, but of course, planes existed when I was alive. I don't know what would happen to him. We need a handbook."

Bella agreed. "What about a cruise ship? Would he travel by boat?"

"Brilliant!" Lena said. "I don't know why I never thought of that. Of course, you'd have the perfect answer." She smiled at Bella. "Tell me why you're here."

Bella gave Lena an abbreviated version of her mission.

"What's so special about this guy? Why do you want Daniel?" Lena asked.

Bella adjusted her sunglasses, stretched one long brown leg further on the chaise, and sank deeper into the cushion.

"Number one, I love him."

"Okay."

"Number two, the dating pool for ghosts is no different from reality."

Lena laughed.

"Who did you marry?" Bella asked sharply.

"My college boyfriend the summer after we graduated."

"My point. You don't know what it means to date. After I eliminate all the men who are trying to reconnect with their wives and men under twenty-five, there's no one left. There are really old men in their sixties, seventies, and eighties and there's no reason to be with them given that money isn't an issue. So, I want Daniel. He's handsome and smart. I know the sex is good. I don't want some other ghost claiming him. He's mine."

"But he left you. Twice."

"Once, really. I knew he wouldn't come to Europe if I didn't tell him about the baby. The second time was out of fear. He fell apart when his father died. Guilt is his driving emotion. He felt guilty that his father knew about the two of us. He's also superstitious. He may have thought he was being punished for the affair and if he didn't stay with his wife, something worse would happen."

"He got that wrong."

"Most certainly. He'd forgotten he owed me honesty, above all else." Bella drew her wide-brimmed sunhat lower over her eyes. "I also want to get him now before he diminishes physically. It's bad enough his hair is white. At least he has a good cut. He was inactive for a while, but he's back to daily runs. Once I finish the court case, I'll swoop in." She snapped her fingers. "*Voilà*! Mine again. Forever."

"How do you know it's forever? How does it work?" Unlike Bella, Lena was married when she died. She didn't understand the need to reconnect with romantic partners.

"Once I get what I want—a Daniel who dies by anything other than natural causes so he'll become a ghost—we'll be together forever. That's the rule."

"What if he doesn't want to be with you? I mean, you did frame him for murder."

"He has no memory of that. He never stopped loving me. We've always wanted to spend eternity together. Now, we will." She shrugged.

Lena rearranged herself on her chaise. "What

about the man you're with here? Mark? He's hot."

"Yes, but he's human. He'll make someone a great husband. He's thirty-five and just recognizing his potential. He has a happy life ahead of him."

"But…" Lena prodded.

"He's too dependent on me. I got him away from Richmond for the weekend so he can relax, see there's more to life than the Country Club of Virginia, and be fresh for court Monday morning. He's a work in progress. I don't want to take that on."

"He's handsome, though."

Bella eyed her friend. "Lena, if you're interested, feel free. Otherwise, find a nice living woman in London and arrange for them to meet."

Lena laughed.

Bella turned the subject back to Lena and her husband. "Where's William?"

"We alternate visiting the girls. He loves seeing them, but he doesn't know what to look for in growing girls. He thinks his sister is a perfectly good substitute parent. He's blind to any faults she might have."

"How do you intervene?" Bella was curious. She'd improvised her interactions with humans.

"Depends upon the situation. When it was time for them to enroll in school, I called the enrollment office where I wanted them to attend and had an application sent. I told the admissions officer they were Legacies so she'd be certain to follow up.

"I rely on being invisible. I remove things in the house I don't think the girls should have and I leave notes in their aunt's handwriting. I've become quite good at forgery."

Bella laughed. "We ghosts have to resort to crime to accomplish things. I'm quite a good thief."

They chatted about their techniques over drinks they poured out when no one was looking. "When do you plan to retire?" Bella asked.

"We don't know. William wants to see them married. I want to see them turn eighteen. After that, they're beyond parental influence. They're eleven."

"That's a long time. I find it tiring to be visible for long periods. I'll be glad to go."

"We have the advantage of being two who can switch off. Also, supervising doesn't require us to be visible too often. I wouldn't be visible now if we hadn't met."

"It's been lovely to see you, Lena. I haven't had a good ghost-to-ghost chat in ages."

***

Sunday morning was time for sleeping late, rolling around in bed, and reading the paper. Mark was delighted that *The Royal Gazette* covered cricket and soccer. "I wish we could stay another day. I'd like to play golf again."

"Sorry, but you have a court date tomorrow morning," Bella reminded him as she rolled over to face him in their bed with tangled sheets.

"Don't you think Opal could handle it?" He grinned.

"Probably. She'll make you obsolete if given free rein."

"Sounds good to me," he said as he nuzzled her neck. "She can take over the firm and you and I can travel the world."

Bella silently slid her right hand under the sheets. Although she didn't like to be the aggressor with Mark, Bella wanted to avoid a discussion of the future. She had a tan, handsome, virile man in her bed now and she wasn't going to waste an opportunity for a deliciously satisfying romp. Mark responded vigorously before smoothly switching to a more languid pace. Bella enjoyed all of it. She had no self-consciousness about her body or her sexual prowess. When they were sated, Mark lay on his stomach with his left arm flung across Bella's body and slept. Bella rested.

About one o'clock, Bella woke Mark. "Hey, it's time to go. We need showers and lunch."

Mark reluctantly sat upright.

"That, Bella, makes me want you in my life even more."

She shushed him as she ordered room service.

While they waited, Mark returned to the topic Bella had hoped to avoid—the future. "I get it. We don't need to close the office so you and I can travel the world. You've already done that. Bella, you're thirty-one and you've lived three lifetimes more than I have. How is that? Why do I feel so far behind?"

"Mark," she said kindly without condescension, "we're different people and want different things." She swung her legs across the bed and onto the floor. "You know the French novelist Émile Zola?"

He nodded.

"When I was very young, I read his quote: 'I am here to live out loud.' That inspired me to live my life as I do—out loud. I always wanted to travel as part of my life. I couldn't wait to get out of Virginia Beach for college and from Charlottesville to Paris. From there, the world was open to me. I pursued it. You were content with a life in Richmond until recently."

"When I realized how much of an outsider I am. You showed me that. You showed me I can do more. I don't have to live a circumscribed life. In just the few days we've been here, I've golfed with a Scotsman, sailed with a South African couple, and played croquet with two Indian guys. I've never met such exotic people."

Bella uttered her joyous, melodious laugh. "Mark, they're not exotic. They all have roots somewhere in the British Empire. You share a common language and interests. All that's missing is some Canadians and Australians."

He looked pensive. "Australians. I've never visited my sister in Sydney. She's been there more than ten years and I haven't seen her. It never occurred to me to visit. I had no curiosity about where or how she lived. I'd like to go now. After the trial. What do you say?"

Bella headed to the shower. "I say you should go," she called over her shoulder before he could invite her to travel with him. She didn't want a disagreement to distract him from the work before him. Tomorrow's court appearance was important.

CHAPTER THIRTY-FIVE

Monday morning, the deputy attorney general himself argued the motion to postpone the trial. Normally, this would be done by a staff attorney, but apparently the office wanted to demonstrate the seriousness of their intent.

Mark, alone at the plaintiff's table, rose to argue against postponement. The plaintiffs had conducted discovery, including depositions, of more than 120 witnesses, reviewed the murder trial transcript, and received reports from expert witnesses. He was prepared for trial.

There had been no amended complaint, no new evidence, and no outstanding matters regarding the case that would be reason to postpone. Most importantly, Evan Cooper's family would be harmed by the delay. They had waited two years for the murder trial and sentencing of their son's killer. There was no need to further prolong their wait for justice.

Bella, who sat invisibly at the back of the courtroom, silently applauded. Mark was great in court. Knowledgeable, quick, and serious. Handsome.

Judge King questioned the deputy AG until she was satisfied. "Mr. Deputy Attorney General, could you please explain why your office with its two hundred attorneys has been unable to depose no more than five witnesses when plaintiff's counsel, who is a solo practitioner, has completed discovery, including the deposition, of more than one hundred witnesses?"

"I can't speak for the plaintiff's counsel. The AG's office has an enormous caseload and is understaffed."

"Has the number of cases or attorneys changed since the plaintiff's complaint was filed?"

"I don't know, Your Honor." He desperately turned to the lawyers behind him at the defense table. None of them met his eyes.

"Did you have any Reductions in Force or mass exodus of staff, Mr. Deputy Attorney General?" she prompted.

"No, Your Honor."

"Mr. Deputy Attorney General, your office didn't make an appearance at the scheduling conference for this case." She sent him a sharp look that demanded explanation.

"Your Honor, the attorney general and the staff were in shock at the allegations against Judge Whiting."

"So shocked as to neglect your duties to the people of the Commonwealth? To neglect to send even the lowest ranking staff attorney to the conference?"

"Your Honor, none of the missed appearances were intentional." Bella noted that the back of his neck had turned red with embarrassment.

"I'm glad you mentioned appearances—plural. Your office missed three appearances in this court that day. Notice of misconduct has been filed with the Office of Professional Responsibility."

Ethics violations. If so inclined, the ethics committee could sanction or even disbar anyone reported by Judge King.

The deputy AG blanched and didn't respond.

"After the office recovered from the shock of Judge Whiting's loathsome activities, why didn't you file a motion to amend the schedule?"

A young woman rose to address the court. "May it please the court."

"Yes, Ms. Kellogg, can you explain the apparent laxness in the AG's office?"

"Your Honor, several senior attorneys were taken out of rotation in order to handle any matters that might arise from Judge Whiting's death. Some cases may have slipped through the cracks in rescheduling."

"Thank you, Ms. Kellogg." Judge King refocused her attention on the Deputy AG.

"Mr. Deputy Attorney General, your office has played fast and loose with the Federal Rules of Civil Procedure. United States attorneys in offices under the jurisdiction of the Fourth Circuit Court of Appeals managed the impact of Judge Whiting's death without assistance from the Virginia attorney general. You've had ample time to raise any objections, complete discovery, and be prepared for trial in two weeks. I order the original trial date to stand."

Mark, who had remained silent with no show of emotion on his face throughout Judge King's questioning, merely nodded and said, "Thank you, Your Honor."

Judge King wasn't finished. "I'm also sanctioning the attorney general and the deputy attorney general personally for failure to raise the proper motions at the proper time and for bringing this frivolous motion today.

"I'm not going to award a default judgment in favor of the plaintiff although I would be well within my powers to do so because the people of the Commonwealth deserve to be heard on this matter. Sanctions will be court costs plus $15,000 payable by the end of the business day to plaintiff for attorney's fees. Adjourned."

***

"That was awesome," Opal said as she walked out of the courthouse with Mark. She'd asked to attend the hearing to see if it was anything like TV courtroom dramas. She'd dressed conservatively in a navy blazer that hit her mid-thigh, navy and white pinstriped tights, and red suede platform shoes.

"I can't believe how Judge King schooled the deputy attorney general. I thought he was going to faint with embarrassment. I didn't know judges could do that. What did she mean about the plaintiffs getting $15,000?"

Mark nodded to a few attorneys he knew as they walked back to the office. "He dissed her when no one from his office showed up for a scheduling conference after Judge Whiting's murder. That's a huge mistake and against the rules. She could've issued a verdict in favor of us right then, but she knew she'd be overturned on appeal and as she said, the Commonwealth does have a right to provide a defense against our accusations. So, she fined them fifteen thousand dollars, which is what she estimated my expenses were today."

"Fifteen thousand dollars for today?" Opal whispered in awe.

"It was more of a fine than a true estimate of my services."

"Do you keep the money?"

"I'll put it in an escrow account. When we win, the judge will award a certain amount for expenses in addition to the damages—we've asked for twenty million dollars for Evan Cooper's family. I'll use that fifteen thousand dollars to pay some of the actual expenses. Of course, Judge King might order Commonwealth to pay all expenses so that would just be added to the amount the Coopers receive."

"Twenty million dollars. How did you come up with that amount?" Opal was talking and walking so fast Mark almost thought she was high.

"In cases like these, the law requires us to put a value on human life. Nineteen million dollars is one million for every year of Evan's life. An extra million is requested as a penalty."

"There's like a formula to calculate what a

person is worth?"

"No, we look at other amounts awarded in similar cases and ask for about the same thing. There weren't really any cases like this so Bella came up with something that seemed reasonable. The judge doesn't have to abide by the number. They usually lower it."

"I had no idea judges had so much juice. How do you get to be a judge? Do you have to be a lawyer first? Why aren't you a judge, Mark?"

Mark's ringing phone saved him from further discussion.

CHAPTER
THIRTY-SIX

"Change of plans," Mark called to Bella when he got back from court. "Dr. Constantine called to say we can depose Larry Yarbrough. He's alert enough to speak and know he's under oath. He's in organ failure, so we need to get there as soon as we can."

Opal stepped into Mark's office. "I checked the airlines. Nothing non-stop. Unbelievable. You have to go to Atlanta to get to Raleigh/Durham. The drive is about two and a half hours. The only full-service hotel near the hospital is the Hilton. The concierge at the hospital can arrange your rooms. Should I make that happen?"

"Yes." Mark answered before Bella had a chance to speak.

"The concierge will arrange transportation to the hospital so you won't have to worry about parking. Dr. Constantine said you should be there at ten o'clock tomorrow morning. Anything else?"

"Yes, Opal. Please see that there's a court

214

reporter available to be at the hospital at that time," Bella said.

Mark looked at his watch and then Bella. "Do you need to get anything from home?"

"No, I always carry a change of clothes in my bag. I don't need anything else if you're taking your laptop."

"Okay. I have to stop by my house, but it's on the way. I want to finish these motions and get on the road," Mark said. "Opal, you're in charge."

***

Bella waited impatiently until they reached the North Carolina state line. Virginia was so strict on speeding that traffic crawled along the highway. As soon as they were in North Carolina, Mark could open up the car. She wondered if she was addicted to speeding in fast cars. Cars had never mattered in New York or Paris or the south of France. She loved flying down the highway.

"Want to drive?" Mark asked.

"No driver's license," she yelled over the wind. *Yes, yes, yes.* She wanted to drive, but she was a ghost. She couldn't concentrate on being visible and driving.

"I've never heard of that."

"Never needed one. I know how to drive, I just don't."

They pulled up in front of the hotel in just over two hours. Mark had flown down I-95. The hospital concierge had booked a suite on a corporate floor where patients' families weren't located. He explained patients and their families tended to prefer to be away from business travelers. He offered to make a dinner reservation for them in the hotel dining room. Bella demurred.

"You're not hungry?"

"I thought I'd take a swim and grab something in the fitness café."

"Well, I need a steak. Maybe I should order room service."

She kissed him. "Whatever you want. I'll be back in about an hour."

Bella loved water. She loved the feel of moving through it even as a ghost. She'd been surprised her ghostly body could swim. It was one of the first things she'd tried when she became an active ghost. The worst that could happen was she'd learn her limits. She couldn't drown. She'd grown up with the Atlantic Ocean as her back yard in Virginia Beach. Her childhood summers and holidays were spent at the family house in St. John. There was nothing better than a salty swim and being kissed by the sun. Thanks to her mother's insistence she wear a hat, her skin remained free of sun damage. Regular skin treatments as an adult had kept her body silky smooth.

Alone at the pool, Bella swam underwater laps. She felt a rush of tranquility when she first put her head under the water and pushed off. Because she didn't need to breathe, Bella rolled and tumbled and somersaulted under the water as long as she wanted. Before she got out, Bella did ballet *barre* exercises, holding onto the side of the pool with her fingertips. She concentrated on her movements and shut out the sound of traffic on the other side of the pool fence.

In the ladies' locker room, Bella sat alone in the steam room. The warm, moist water rising from cedar felt delicious. She luxuriated there for what seemed like moments before her twenty-minute timer sounded. She got out, dressed in an oversized Duke University Hospital jersey that brushed her knees, and stopped by the small café. She plucked a boxed salad, an apple, and a flavored iced tea from the chilled display case and charged them to the room. She couldn't eat, but Mark would see she'd bought it.

She took the express elevator to their floor. Mark, wearing his suit pants and a blue oxford shirt with his sleeves rolled up, was eating his favorite meal of steak and baked potato and watching something on the Syfy channel. "*The Martian* is coming on. I missed it in the movie theatres. What do you say?"

She sat on the arm of his chair. "I say I'm going to review the Larry Yarbrough trial transcript and initial assessment by Dr. Constantine. I might tweak the depo questions."

His hand traveled up her silky leg to her thigh. "Do you ever wear panties?"

"Of course. I thought I'd wear them tomorrow at the hospital. No need for them after a swim."

He pushed the dinner tray aside and pulled her onto his lap. "You are the most gorgeous, wild, and single-minded woman I've met. I must have been under a lucky star when you walked into Beacon's that night." He kissed her with a promise of more and she scooted off his lap.

"I'll be in Bedroom Number One if you need me," she teased and closed the door.

In the solitude of the room, she re-read the key points of Larry Yarbrough's murder trial. He was a prime example of when a Not Guilty by Reason of Insanity plea should be used. His public defender never raised it. Yarbrough would never live long enough for an appeal.

She read what little there was on his background from a social services report. Laid off from a construction job. Turned to drugs and alcohol. Lived with his younger sister and her husband until he started taking dangerous drugs. After that, he drifted from score to score, most likely unaware of where he was or what he did. Drugs had seduced, conquered, and were now killing him.

Dr. Constantine's written assessment confirmed what he'd said by phone. Bath salts had kidnapped Larry's heart, kidney, and liver. He had significant cognitive damage and memory loss. If they could get anything that would implicate the state in Evan Cooper's murder, their case was won.

CHAPTER

THIRTY-SEVEN

"Hey, why so sad?" Mark asked when he sat beside her and dimmed the lights. She'd been reading on the bed with the transcripts propped on her knees.

"Is the movie over already?" She hadn't been reading that long.

"Why would I watch a movie I can see any time when I have a hot woman in the bedroom who must be close to finishing work for the day?"

"I see your point. Glad to hear I beat out Matt Damon."

He laughed. "It was a close call, but you're prettier. He hasn't aged well." He ran his hands up one smooth thigh.

Bella laughed her siren's laugh. "He's also about fifteen years older than I am."

"Really?" Mark said. He leaned back against the headboard. "I basically know nothing about you."

Bella got off the bed and put the files neatly in

her briefcase. "You know what matters."

"Like?" Half question. Half challenge.

She sat on the bed and stretched out her legs. "I'm brilliant, ruthless according to you, and an exceptional lover."

He made his crinkly eyed laugh. "Modest. You didn't mention modesty or humility."

"You know I possess neither of those qualities," she said as she turned to face him. "They're highly overrated. I prefer honest to disingenuous."

"So, that's it? That's all there is to you?"

"I don't talk about myself. It's not important."

"But it's important for you to tell me that I need to create a home, find a wife, and broaden my horizons," he said amiably.

She poked him in the ribs. "You asked."

"Touché. I might have amazing insights. Try me."

She looked directly into his eyes. "Mark, my life is just as I want it. I have no one to please but myself. That makes me selfish. There are worse things to be."

He seemed surprised by her candor. "Well, at least tell me why you're suddenly available."

"I decided to be available to you. You're a hard man to resist. Why should I deprive myself? That's the selfishness speaking."

"Your life isn't just like you want it if you're making adjustments," he suggested as he ran his hand along her leg.

"New opportunities present themselves all the time. If I didn't make adjustments, I'd be in a rut or worse."

"Like me, you mean." He looked serious.

"You're being ridiculous." She made an exaggerated sigh. "You can have one question. What do you want to know? Favorite color? Animal? Vacation spot?"

He turned her head to face him. "Why isn't someone as fabulous as you married?"

"I was," she said quietly and without hesitation. "He died of cancer when I was thirty."

She closed her eyes for just a moment to get the image of seeing her handsome, brilliant, and vibrant husband waste away. He hadn't wanted any futile interventions, but even reducing or eliminating pain and keeping him comfortable hastened his physical decline. She was grateful his mind had never been affected.

Mark cursed. "I'm sorry." He banged his head against the headboard. "I'm sorry I pushed you into telling me something painful."

She'd successfully pushed all the horrible images back in the deepest recesses of her mind.

"It's part of who I am, Mark. It changed me. I learned to live with pain. It's not something I volunteer," she said. "Law school 101. Never ask a question you don't know or want the answer to. Grammatically incorrect, but that's the rule."

"Man, I am an idiot."

She laughed to lighten the mood. She didn't want a serious conversation. She wanted sex and for Mark to sleep. They'd both need iron spines tomorrow.

CHAPTER
THIRTY-EIGHT

The bald man in the hospital bed looked nothing like the violent hulk repeatedly shown on Richmond TV stations. This man, sitting with the head of the bed raised, looked robbed of life and substance. His skin and the whites of his eyes were yellow from liver failure. Three separate IV tubes curled around each other from a central catheter embedded in his chest. Both of his hands were swollen and bluish purple from previous IV injections. His cheeks were sunken with excess skin from the larger man he'd once been resting on his face. He was sedated to be calm but responsive. He was soon to be put into a medically induced coma to better attend and relieve his physical failings.

Bella reminded herself they just needed to get what they needed and get out. When she and Mark arrived, Dr. Constantine recited the facts of his medical condition, the medications he was receiving, and the date, time, and location of the deposition for the record. He then woke Larry Yarbrough. On the record, Mark and Bella introduced themselves. Mark wanted Bella to do the questioning on the slight chance that a female voice would elicit calm, focused responses.

"Mr. Yarbrough, do you know where you are now?" she said with quiet authority.

"Hospital." There was a hoarseness in his voice from medication or lung damage. Bella didn't know. She didn't want to know. The goal was to get what they needed and leave him.

"Do you remember being in a hospital in Virginia?"

"Sorta'."

"Was it bright, like this one? Did you have the same number of doctors and nurses?"

"Dark. No docs."

"Why were you in the hospital in Virginia?"

"High."

"On what?"

He stuck his white tongue out to lick his dry, cracked lips. "Bath salts." Bella willed herself not to show her revulsion.

"You took bath salts a lot?"

"Oh, yeah. Do you have some? Did you bring me some?" His eyes had a brief glint of interest at the prospect of drugging himself out of the moment. She ignored his look.

"No, Mr. Yarbrough. In the Virginia hospital, were you alone in a room?"

"Too hot. Too hot in there. Had to keep looking for a fan that worked."

"Where were the fans?"

"A room down the hall. All lying down. Wouldn't stay upright. Just threw them on the floor. No plug anyway. I needed an air-conditioner. Couldn't find one. Ripped up the room looking for it."

"You weren't locked in your room?"

"Too hot."

"Did anyone help you look for a fan or an air-conditioner?"

"No. Watched me but didn't help."

"Who watched you?" This was the critical question. Once he answered, she could leave.

"The man behind the glass. He had keys to air-conditioners. I banged on glass, threw chair at glass. It wouldn't break."

"You asked for help and no one helped you. Is that correct?"

"Yes."

"Do you remember how long you looked for something to cool your room?"

"Days. Couldn't sleep. Too hot. Too hot."

"Did you ever cool down?"

"When I found my salts."

"You had bath salts in the hospital?" She couldn't let this oddity get her off track. Stick with verifying the tape. Get what he recalled of the night.

"Yes, snuck them in. No search."

"No search when you were admitted? Did you change clothes?"

"No. Too hot. Just opened the door and pushed me inside."

Bella looked at Mark. He shook his head that he had no questions.

"Mr. Yarbrough, do you know why you're in this hospital?"

"Bath salts."

"Do you feel the same way as you did in the Virginia hospital?"

"No, bath salts are killing me now."

"You believe you're dying?"

"I know. Heart hurts. Can't breathe."

"Did you tell me the truth?"

"Sure."

"Thank you, Mr. Yarbrough."

Bella stepped back from the bed, left the room, and dictated the formalities to the court reporter. She went to the end of the hall and took the elevator down to the first floor. She wanted to be in the sun and fresh air. She felt like she was cloaked in death.

CHAPTER
THIRTY-NINE

Mark found her sitting on a wooden bench in the hospital courtyard with her jacket off. He had two water bottles with him. He sat next to her, offered her a water, took off his jacket and loosened his tie. His faced was flushed.

"You okay?" he asked Bella.

Keeping up the pretense of physical needs, Bella pressed the cold water bottle against her forehead, throat, and wrists. She nodded her head.

"They all smell alike. Hospitals. Disinfectant and death. Hopelessness and unimaginable pain. Torture, really. Better to skip from diagnosis to death." Bella was talking to herself more than to Mark.

"You think so?"

"I do. Nothing saves us in the end. We get reprieves, but we all die."

Mark sat silently. Bella righted herself. She sounded like an old woman with her talk of despair

226

and death. She focused on the case.

"Opal's pulling the surveillance footage entered into evidence at trial." Before she could explain, her phone buzzed. "That's her." Bella listened before speaking.

"Do you know anyone who can tell where it was altered? Some audio guy or video tech or whatever they're called? Is he reliable? I don't care whether he's stoned. Can he do it? Today. Whatever he usually gets paid plus fifty percent. Thanks."

Mark expected an answer. Bella spelled it out.

"The surveillance tape presented at trial. The so-called authenticated one? Altered if Yarbrough is telling the truth. He said he was checking what he believed to be a storage room, which was most likely Evan Cooper's room and went in and out frequently. He said he asked for help.

"He saw the night nurse, whose name is in the transcript, watching him and not helping him. He banged on the glass. Threw a chair at the glass. None of that was on the tape.

"That nurse sat there and watched Yarbrough in a rage, tear off his clothes, and run around the ward naked looking for something to cool himself. The nurse didn't call anyone. Not even a security guard, unless he shows up on tape. Not a doctor or anyone who could give Yarbrough the elephant tranquilizer that would slow him down, if not knock him out and get him in an ice bath.

"At the height of his episode, Yarbrough was no doubt a wild, dangerous man. So much so that he wasn't searched, made to change into scrubs, or even locked in his room. Whoever made the transfer just let him loose on the ward, where he could prey on whoever his drug-induced hallucinations suggested. That bastard prosecutor knew. He knew the tapes were altered. He wanted Yarbrough to be guilty without raising the issue of the state's culpability. Disbarment isn't enough. I want to grind a hole in his filthy hands with my stilettos."

Mark stood and cursed. He paced in the sun.

"Another one. All these old boys are corrupt. Dinwiddie County isn't a prestigious assignment, but the prosecutor is an old boy. About five years ahead of me at UVA Law. How could I not see it? He's an arrogant ass, but I didn't think he'd tamper with evidence in a murder case."

Bella tried to be soothing. "For corruption to work, there has to be old boys in all places, not just the prestigious ones."

Mark nodded and moved on. "I take it Opal is having the tape reviewed by an expert so we know where and how much it was edited?"

Bella nodded. "I also asked if the tech can determine whether the audio track is missing versus never recorded. My guess is it was cut. The jury saw Yarbrough screaming and ranting, but didn't hear his words.

"Mark, once Opal's guy finishes, we need to subpoena the entire surveillance footage for that night. We need to let her obtain it through her connections. Getting it through proper channels isn't going to work. They'll stall us."

"You're right. We'll go through the motions just like we did with documents and retrieve them ourselves. Damn, you're good. Are you a hundred times smarter than me or is it objectivity? An outsider looking in?"

"A little of each. Plus I work with corruption. I'm trained to look for it. I'm not a cynic. A realist."

"Wow," Mark said. "Just wow."

CHAPTER FORTY

Bella wanted to fly in the car all the way back to Richmond. Instead, they shot through North Carolina and slowed on I-95 north of the Virginia state line. After taking Larry Yarbrough's deposition, Mark and Bella went back to the hotel. Mark had lunch. Bella swam.

She called a personal shopper at Saks in Richmond and requested that a particular dress for which she knew the style number be delivered to Mark's community concierge during the afternoon or evening. She intended to wear her Duke Hospital jersey with cheap sandals also purchased at the gift shop home. She threw the suit she'd worn to the deposition in the trash.

She called Opal and told her they were on their way back. Bella wasn't coming into the office. Mark might. Opal hadn't yet heard from the tech reviewing the evidentiary tape.

"Are you wearing that home?" Mark asked when he saw Bella in her jersey and sandals.

"Yes, I had to get that suit off. I felt like it was

crawling with lies and death and hate."

"That's why you took a swim."

She nodded.

"What about what you wore yesterday?"

"It's in my bag. Just needs to be cleaned." She was desperate to get out of there. "Mark, I'll meet you downstairs. I need to be outside."

Bella jumped in the car almost before it stopped when the valet brought it to the front of the hotel. She put on a scarf and sunglasses and said, "Let's go."

They drove in silence, mostly because of the noise of the wind and traffic. Bella didn't feel completely free of revulsion until they pulled into Mark's garage. She raced upstairs, put on her silk satin robe, and pulled her hair into a knot at the top of her head. Some blonde tendrils drifted along her cheekbones.

Mark came upstairs. "I take it you're not going back to the office."

"No, this morning did me in. I spoke to Opal. No word yet from the tech guy."

"I'm going in for a couple of hours. Make some calls. Check email. All things I could do here, but I want to show my face."

"And make sure Opal's not having a rave in the office?" she said to lighten the mood.

"Something like that." He hesitated before he spoke. "Bella, whatever tape was entered into evidence at trial is stored along with all the other evidence in the Dinwiddie County courthouse."

"Yes," Bella said, "that's where the tech guy, using your signature, checked it out. He's reviewing it on equipment in the courthouse. It can't be removed from the building without a court order."

Mark didn't remark on the use of his signature to obtain evidence. "The techie is certain that it's been altered?"

Bella nodded.

"So falsified evidence was admitted at trial. The original tape never made it to trial. It's either with the police or it's gone missing. Somewhere in the Petersburg police or Dinwiddie County Sherriff's evidence room is a box full of stuff that wasn't entered into the court record. The original tape is physically in that box."

"If we make a formal request, it will definitely go missing." Bella thought aloud.

Mark shook his head. "Maybe not. This was done by the prosecutor's office. He wouldn't be stupid enough to involve the police. Cops have really tightened up their evidence logs. They can't afford to let rape kits, cigarette butts, and anything that might have a speck of DNA on it go missing. Ten years ago, maybe. Not now."

"Do you have any friends on the force in Petersburg?"

"I do. I have to decide whether to involve her. I don't want to get her disciplined or fired."

"Well, think about it."

Mark walked toward her and pulled her close. "Are you going to nap?"

"Probably." She was too wound up to nap, but she might rest. Even become invisible for a while.

He tucked one of the tendrils of her hair behind her ear. "Bella, you were amazing. You got what we need in less than fifteen minutes. We can't help Larry Yarbrough. We're looking at a bigger picture."

She nodded.

"Part of the bigger picture is you and me. I want you in my life. Not just professionally. Personally. We have something undeniable. You're a dream for me."

His mouth found hers. She was tempted to fling open her robe and delay his return to the office. Pressing against him was enough. He was solid and strong. Nothing sickly or frail about him. She needed that. She wanted him, but she wasn't going to lose focus or delay him.

She'd seen death today. Dr. Constantine had called Mark to say Larry Yarbrough had died three hours after they left. They'd probably just gotten off the highway when he died. They'd almost missed their chance with him. Still, Bella couldn't shake the picture of that dying man.

Bella put her hands on Mark's chest and pulled away from him. "Go. Do what you need to do. Opal knows what we need and she's the liaison with the tech guy. I wouldn't understand him."

Mark kissed her on the cheek. "Aha. You're aren't all-knowing. You're not a techie."

Bella smiled and watched him leave. If he only knew. Her recent education was how to be a ghost who could be visible, invisible, and space travel at will. Her tech skills hadn't been updated since her death in 2001. She'd had to read the entire manual twice in order to use that genius phone system Opal had installed. Texting was her limit.

With Mark out of the house, Bella lay on the bed and let big, choking sobs escape from her. She cried for all her losses. Daniel, her parents, her husband, and the three hundred seventy-two colleagues, clients, and friends in the World Trade Center on September 11, 2001. She cried for Evan Cooper and Larry Yarbrough and all the souls still not at rest in Commonwealth Psych. She cried until there was nothing left in her. She was empty. She wanted to finish this case and move on to eternity with Daniel.

Daniel. The man she'd loved since she was seventeen years old. His mind and body had failed him, but he was trying so hard to get better. He hadn't given up. She couldn't give him up, either.

CHAPTER

FORTY-ONE

Dressed in the hot pink wool dress she'd had delivered to Mark's concierge, Bella reviewed the information provided by Opal's tech. According to his analysis, the tape had been altered seven times. He had marked the nanoseconds almost immediately after the introduction, four times during the first twenty minutes, and twice during the last five.

She was glad she hadn't gone to the office yesterday afternoon. Bella pretended to be asleep when Mark returned just after seven o'clock. She'd taken the news of Larry Yarbrough's death hard. She'd literally taken his dying declaration and needed to take a break before tackling what could be key evidence this morning. She'd deliberately worn a vibrant color as a reminder to remain focused on the case and not let grief overcome her. She had eternity with Daniel in her near future.

The tech's report described the editing of the

surveillance video as clumsy and amateurish to a professionally trained eye. He estimated the bulk of a seven-hour shift to be missing. His opinion was that the audio track had been extracted by software available to download for free. Nothing that had been done required technical expertise.

"What do you think?" Opal sat on the sofa in Mark's office with Bella. Mark was doing physician depositions in the conference room.

"Good job. Do you understand how any of this works?"

"Sure. I sometimes hang with the DJ at clubs."

Bella wondered if Opal had a social life outside clubs. She probably knew LouLou, but wasn't going to ask her.

"Walk me through how this would be done. Assume I know nothing."

"Do you know anything?"

"No." Bella laughed. "Not a thing."

"It's easy. A surveillance camera is hooked up to a DVR. If there are multiple cameras, they can go to the same DVR. If you want to review the footage, you just play the DVR like you would for a recorded TV show. It's not accurate to call it surveillance video anymore. It's digital. It can be saved on a USB."

"You mean a regular DVR used at home?"

"Yes. Nothing fancy. The DVR can be on site or remote. In the hospital, it would be on site. Anyone sitting in front of it could see multiple cameras simultaneously. My buddy was surprised the hospital even had digital recording. He said most older government buildings still use video cassettes."

"Could a video be transferred to digital for editing?"

"Yes. He said it might have happened in this case because the quality of the black and white video was poor for a prime digital recording."

"And the sound?"

"Same thing. It's on the DVR. A free download can separate audio and visual. Some DVRs have that feature built in."

"Opal, check the transcripts for anything about video surveillance. Who testified? How many surveillance cameras there were? What kind of recorder? Anything. Also, get the authenticity stipulation. "

"What's that?"

"A document that states the prosecution and defense agree that a piece of evidence is what it's supposed to be. An expert examines it and says it's real. Like OJ's glove."

Opal looked at her expectantly.

"Never mind. You're not old enough. Just copy or print the exhibit page about surveillance video."

Bella leaned back on the sofa, closed her eyes, and planned her next move.

CHAPTER

FORTY-TWO

"You're related to LouLou Fleming, aren't you?" asked the Sensitive at the only music store in Richmond. Bella was startled. She hadn't seen him when she came in. Her attention had been drawn to the gorgeous black cat stretched on the front counter. She couldn't keep her hands off him and he obliged by rolling over so she could stroke all of him.

"I'm Skylar, the proprietor of Vinyl. I see you've established a friendship with my partner, Robert."

"He's so handsome," Bella said as she turned on her considerable charms. "You must have women coming in all the time just to see him."

"Mmm," Skylar said in a noncommittal tone.

"Is he named for the great bluesman Robert Lee Johnson?" she asked with her gorgeous blue eyes trained on Skylar.

"Why yes, he is. Are you a blues fan?" the old man asked.

238

"I love many kinds of music, but the blues hold some very good memories for me."

"And LouLou?" Skylar wasn't going to let her wriggle out of that.

"Ms. Fleming is a witness in one of my cases. I took her deposition a few weeks ago, which brings me to why I'm here. I have an odd request, but I couldn't think of where else I might find something. I need a VHS tape."

"What kind?"

"Musical. I realize you don't sell films here, but operas and concerts were recorded on them before the world went digital." She sighed as though downloads signaled the end of civilization.

"You don't have any preference as to what's on it?" Skylar asked.

Bella slowly stroked her cheek to her chin with her index finger as she pretended to think. "I'd love Puccini's *Turandot*. Do you have it with Pavarotti singing the role of Calaf? Any soprano is fine. Joan Sutherland or Monserrat Caballé would be ideal."

"Yes, I have that with Sutherland. I'll get it. Robert will keep an eye on you." Skylar headed toward a row of VHS tapes on one shelf at the far corner of the store. Bella wondered if she should be concerned. Then again, what could he possibly do? Tell LouLou she'd been to his store and when asked, she'd admitted to taking a deposition. Of course, with LouLou, anything could set her off on a psychotic episode.

"Here you are," said a brusque Skylar. He moved Robert enough to place the tape on the counter. "The price is on the box. Is there anything else?"

"No, thank you." She took cash out of her briefcase to pay. When she put her hand out to take the tape, Skylar put his hand on hers. She forced herself not to flinch.

"You're Bella, aren't you?" he asked.

She took the tape with her free hand and put it in her briefcase. "Yes, I am," she said briskly.

Skylar stood straighter. Almost as if he were prepared to physically do battle for LouLou.

"I've no reason to deny it. I'm here solely for the purpose of obtaining the tape. I'm not stalking LouLou. You can tell her I was here and upset her or keep this to yourself. It's up to you. I don't plan to see either of you again."

Skylar relaxed his shoulders and removed his hand from hers. "LouLou showed me the book you gave her. She's been trying to relive every moment with Gregg so she can include it in the list of places he might return." He absent-mindedly rubbed Robert's head.

"Skylar, I can't help her. I don't know where Gregg is or how she can reach him. I taught myself what I need to function as a ghost on earth. There's no guide."

"That's too bad." Skylar shook his head. "Seems like there should be some sort of ghost oral history passed around."

Bella nodded but didn't speak.

"I don't mean to sound disloyal, but you're an exceptionable woman. You are the most gorgeous woman I've ever seen, not that that's pertinent to Gregg. The point is you're brilliant, well-educated, and sophisticated." He hesitated. "LouLou's Gregg

240

is a musical genius, but I don't think he has a great intellect and he has no education beyond high school. He died in the 1980s and was hospitalized in the late 1960s so he's almost fifty years behind in everything. Technology, social mores, and transportation. If he didn't find eternal peace and is trying to come back to LouLou, he's at a great disadvantage."

"Skylar," she said softly, "I'm back because I willed myself to be. I came back for Daniel—LouLou's father. My return has nothing to do with intelligence. It's raw emotion. Stinging, searing, slashing pain embedded in my heart. If Gregg feels that for LouLou, he'll learn whatever he needs. LouLou can only wait. Gregg has to return if he can. I don't know him so I can't predict whether he'll be able to find his way back."

Skylar would know if there was even a chance of Gregg returning. "Do you think he left prematurely?" Bella asked. "LouLou said he had music still inside him."

Skylar eyed her with suspicion. "Yes, I think he left rather too quickly. He had plenty of music in his head."

Bella wasn't going to belabor talk about Gregg's departure with a Sensitive. He couldn't read her mind, but Skylar might suspect she had something to do with Gregg's premature exit. She stroked Robert one last time.

"Skylar, you're the one who can help her. You have the ability to divine several dimensions simultaneously and you know both LouLou and Gregg. I wish you the best."

241

As she put her hand on the doorknob, Robert let out a long, loud, Siamese cry. Bella knew he was sorry to see her go.

CHAPTER

FORTY-THREE

Mark was disappointed she wouldn't spend the night with him, but Bella allowed him to take her to dinner. She could pass the time with him before she went on her mission in Petersburg.

They ate at a small family-owned Indian restaurant with low lighting. She allowed Mark to order for them both, but insisted he order his favorites. She wasn't feeling one hundred percent, and assured him that was why she wanted to sleep at home tonight.

"It's the trial, isn't it?" Mark stated as he held her hand across the small table.

"Yes. I knew the hospital was a cesspool, but I didn't realize absolutely everyone we deposed would confirm it. Not one person has said anything positive about patient safety and treatment. Hearing Larry Yarbrough's dying declaration confirmed the worst. I'll feel better once we have the original surveillance tape."

He squeezed her hand. "That will make the case if what Yarbrough remembers is captured on tape. He asked for help and it was denied. Caught on tape, there's no way for the AG to deny it."

Bella nodded and pretended to sip jasmine tea. It smelled lovely and calmed her nerves.

"All assuming what Yarbrough remembers is true and not a hallucination. Besides, we still have to hear what Jess Cox, the aide who was on duty that night and testified at Yarbrough's trial, says tomorrow." She lowered her eyes and looked at him through her long lashes.

"Bella, you don't have to come with me. I can take his deposition alone." He looked genuinely concerned about her.

She looked up at him with tears forming at the creases of her lids. "I must go. I want to get a sense of a man whose job it is to keep patients safe watch a murder be committed without intervening."

"Let me know if you change your mind," Mark said, and he released her hand. Relief at not having to make conversation flooded through Bella.

Mark seemed to relish the medium spicy curry and vegetable filled bread he'd ordered. She was mildly repulsed that he could eat with such gusto.

She pulled off a Bella smile. "The good news is this clinches the case. I'll make a few tweaks to the Motion for Summary Judgment and we're done."

"That's the Bella I know." He smiled.

"Mark, have you been in touch with Evan Cooper's family?"

He nodded while he finished a mouthful. "I called them once a week when the case started, but

Mr. Cooper asked that I just let them know when the trial would start. He and his wife seem to still be in shock that their son is dead even after his murder trial. They don't want details of a civil suit. Mr. Cooper said he wouldn't have retained me if he didn't believe I'd do my best.

"I can't believe I call him Mr. Cooper. He's barely forty. He and Mrs. Cooper were high school sweethearts who married and had a baby young. That baby grew up and is now dead." He shook his head. "Once again, I feel like I'm in a parallel universe to my contemporaries. You, the Coopers, everyone."

"Don't," Bella said more sharply than she'd intended. "Don't make this about you and what you have yet to do with your life. We've got the final damning evidence. We can't make a mistake now that could cost us a win. We both have to keep our wits together. I can't let my rage against the state for the suffering of its patients blind me to what needs to be done. You can worry about your future after we win the Summary Judgment, but we have to win it."

This time, Mark high fived her across the table.

***

Bella left before the check came. She didn't want Mark to offer to see her home. He'd never asked where that home was, although he probably assumed she stayed in a luxury residential hotel. She definitely didn't want him to see her get into a cab headed toward Petersburg.

Once inside the police headquarters, the evidence room should be easy to find. She had a floor plan of the station from the internet. She didn't know how old the plan was, but the building was only two stories and couldn't have been altered significantly. She knew two officers and a clerk were on duty after midnight. They'd never know she was there.

Invisible, she headed where the evidence room was located on the floor plan at the back of the building. There was no duty officer there at one in the morning, but the door was locked. She walked through the wall and discovered rows of overflowing cardboard banker's boxes on shelves from the floor almost to the ceiling. Surely, she wasn't going to have to go through all of them.

A hand printed sign that read **'Media Evidence'** with a drawing of a finger pointing left made her mission easier. The law required media evidence to be housed in a separate location from other crime scene evidence, but she had no expectation that a police department as small as this would actually have complied.

She went to the media room and quickly found the Evan Cooper case file box. She opened it without difficulty and there it was. Lying on top of what looked like computer discs was a VHS tape marked Commonwealth Psychiatric Hospital Surveillance and the date of the murder. She exchanged the VHS copy of *Turandot* she'd purchased at Vinyl for the original surveillance video and left the way she came.

This was it. She had the last piece of evidence in her hand. Bella hadn't wanted to risk someone making the surveillance tape disappear after word got out of Mark's application for a warrant. By substituting *Turandot* for the hospital tape, the surveillance tape was safe with her. Even if someone made the tape disappear, it wouldn't be the surveillance tape; *Turandot* would disappear.

She hadn't let Mark in on her actions. He needed to be able to swear in court that the evidence had been procured lawfully.

Once a warrant for the original video tape was obtained, Mark's friend from the Petersburg police department would go to the evidence room, collect it, and sign the property log. She'd give what she believed to be the surveillance tape to Mark. Everything would be done according to strict chain of custody requirements.

In the meantime, Bella had the real thing.

CHAPTER

FORTY-FOUR

Confident that she had the original surveillance tape in her possession, Bella insisted on accompanying Mark the next afternoon to take the deposition of the aide who had been on duty the night Evan Cooper had been killed. She was surprised that the man still worked at the hospital. Whoever was running the hospital hadn't the foresight to transfer him or retire him or whatever else could be done to get him out of Commonwealth Psychiatric and away from the murder trial or Mark's civil action.

The duo arrived early and waited in a consultation room while security fetched Jess Cox. According to his employment record, Cox was twenty-eight, held a GED, and became a medical assistant or MA through a private online educational service. He'd worked at Commonwealth Psych for six months before the murder. He was single, no criminal record, and had lived his entire life in West Petersburg.

"Ever been here?" Mark asked. He nervously paced the windowless room.

"I'm ashamed to admit I don't want to be here now." She didn't want to be where horrible things took place. She'd had more than enough of that in human form. Bella was here because it was important to get a statement from Cox where he felt most comfortable and where, if necessary, he could walk them through the crime scene. She shivered.

Mark looked out of place. He was far too handsome, well-groomed, and well-dressed to pass even as a physician here.

The door opened and a man in his fifties entered with recording equipment. He was the court reporter for the deposition and looked just as unhappy to be there as Bella and Mark.

Mark tried to put him at ease. "If there's an outlet, try to set up close to the door. You'll want to be able to get out easily for breaks."

The reporter nodded. "I don't know that I want to take a break here. We're on a floor with patients. No one told me we'd be here. What if one of them goes crazy?"

Bella bit the inside of her cheek to prevent her from saying anything. Mark was reassuring. "I think most of these patients are sedated. They're on a locked ward on the other side of the building. Treat it like any other hospital," he said.

After the reporter was set up, the three waited in silence. Cox entered exactly on time.

No one rose to shake his hand. Mark handled the introductions and got the preliminaries on the record. Bella didn't intend to question Cox. She didn't think she'd be able to control her rage at whatever pitiful excuses he might offer.

Mark started the questioning.

"Mr. Cox, you were on duty the night of Evan Cooper's murder, correct?" Mark had stated the date and time of the murder earlier.

"Yes." The young man slouched in his chair. He looked sleepy. Bella wondered if he was stoned although he claimed he hadn't taken any drugs or alcohol prior to the deposition.

"What were your duties that night?"

"That was almost three years ago. I don't know." Bella didn't expect him to play things that way for long. His attempt to stare at her until she became uncomfortable wouldn't work, either. She had the delicious thought of becoming invisible, but that would shock Mark and the court reporter.

"Mr. Cox, you gave a statement to the police at the time of the murder and you were deposed before the murder trial of Larry Yarbrough six months ago. I'll ask you again, what were your duties that shift?"

"Same as always," Cox muttered.

"Itemize them," Mark demanded.

Cox rolled his shoulders and stared at the wall as if he might find an answer there. He finally said, "Cover the shift from seven at night to seven in the morning."

"Mr. Cox, you have a job description, do you not?"

"I dunno."

Mark didn't lose his temper. He signaled the court reporter to stop. "We're going off the record."

Mark leaned forward across the table and spoke directly to Cox. "You're not on the clock. Your shift may end in forty-five minutes, but we don't stop until we're satisfied. You can play games or you can answer truthfully and completely. It's your choice as to how long that takes."

Cox shrugged. "I can use the OT."

"The only person in this room who gets overtime pay is the court reporter. You're here under a judge's order. Failure to comply gets you a night or two in prison until you can be arraigned on contempt charges. Not the Petersburg jail. One of the federal facilities in Hopewell. You'll be in the high or low security prison, whichever has room. I don't care whether your fellow inmates are crooked stock brokers or violent kidnappers because I'm not going to spend time with them. You are. You won't be drawing a paycheck while in prison, Mr. Cox. Now, do we proceed on the record or do I call a federal marshal?"

Mark suddenly had Cox's full attention and cooperation.

"Back on the record."

Mark asked Cox questions about his duties during a shift, the number of patients he oversaw, and what his instructions were if a patient presented a problem. Bella sat quietly. Mark was commanding in his role.

"Under what circumstances was Mr. Yarbrough admitted?"

"What?" Cox's lack of understanding was genuine.

"Who brought him to the ward?" Mark

rephrased.

"Two security officers."

"Is that unusual? Doesn't someone from admitting bring patients back?"

"Yeah, usually it's admitting, but he was really screwed up. Big sucker too. Thrashing and screaming. High on something. Security unlocked the door and shoved him inside."

"Did you go through the usual procedures such as providing him scrubs, taking and inventorying his clothes and personal effects and putting them in a locker, and securing him in his room?"

"Hell, no. I wasn't going to mess with him. He was rabid." Cox's shoulders hunched forward as it trying to protect himself from that memory.

"Did you call someone to report that you had an unstable patient on the ward?"

Cox laughed. "Who would I call? There were always unstable patients on the ward."

"Patients as unstable as Mr. Yarbrough?"

"Not quite as bad as him, but the druggies get adrenaline going and nobody can mess with them."

"No one? Couldn't you call security?" Mark's disbelief was palpable.

"They wouldn't respond." Cox seemed pleased to have insider information on how things worked at Commonwealth Psych.

"Why do you say that?"

"They never do with a druggie. They get him to the hospital and on the ward and that's it."

"Were there specific instances you recall where you had troublesome patients, you called security, and no one responded?"

"Every weekend."

"Is that an exaggeration?" Mark wanted precise answers on the record.

"No, sir." Cox went on a twenty-minute rant of all the times he'd called security and they hadn't come when he first started working there. He eventually learned not to bother them. Employees who disturbed security for junkies had been known to come off shift to find their car tires slashed or their media players missing from the dashboard.

Bella wanted to choke someone. Every avenue of investigation led to another group charged with patient safety who willfully disregarded their duties. She'd thought they'd get enough from Cox to corroborate the longer security tape for which he might face criminal charges. Now, she was hearing that even security turned a blind eye to patients in distress. She was furious that Cox hadn't called security because it was pointless.

Mark had established a rhythm with Cox and wasn't going to take a break. She settled herself to be backup.

"Did Mr. Yarbrough ask for your assistance?"

"He yelled that he was hot. He took off all his clothes and ran around looking for fans. At first, I spoke through the intercom and told him there weren't any fans and the central air-conditioner was on. He wanted a window unit. Like he had a window to put it in. I just put my headphones on and ignored him."

"Mr. Cox, in your experience did Mr. Yarbrough seem better or worse than the usual patient on drugs?"

253

He paused before answering. "Worse. He kept at it for so long. Usually, they wear themselves out after about an hour, but he was like that battery bunny. Going on and on and on."

"Did you call a doctor to sedate him?"

There was that laugh again. "The golden rule is never call the docs. Ever. Well, maybe if the place was burning down. No. I'd call the Fire Department for that. No, we weren't supposed to call the docs."

"Was this a formal policy?"

"You mean like was it written down somewhere?"

"Yes."

"I doubt it. Maybe on a yellow sticky note somewhere, but it was more like insider information. I replaced a girl who'd called a doc for a patient who overdosed. She was terminated because she wasn't capable of making proper assessments. That's how I got hired."

"What about the doctors in the hospital's ER?"

"We never had anything to do with them." Cox looked astonished at the thought of interacting with the ER.

"Back to the night Evan Cooper died. Did you see Mr. Yarbrough go in and out of his room?"

"Sure. He went in everyone's room on that hall."

Bella, who was rarely surprised, was stunned. Daniel had been at risk. Every patient on that ward had been at risk. The surveillance tape had probably been edited to show Yarbrough only going into Evan Cooper's room. She was deep in thought when she realized Mark was speaking to her.

"Do you have any questions for Mr. Cox?"

"Yes," she said. "Did other patients on that ward call you for assistance or medication that night?"

Cox had the grace to look ashamed. "Yes, but I told them to wait until morning. I wasn't going out there with him raging around. I didn't think they should come out of their rooms, either. A missed pill here or there wouldn't make a difference."

"So, you neglected all the other patients because of Mr. Yarbrough?"

"Sure did, ma'am. If you'd have seen him, you'd have done the same thing."

"It was your relief shift that found Mr. Cooper?"

"Yes, three of them came on shift at seven in the morning. I told them they had their hands full. He was still running around buck naked."

"You left at the end of your shift?"

"Yes, ma'am. I was glad to get out of there."

Bella looked at Mark and indicated she had no additional questions. She couldn't stand to hear anymore.

***

Bella and Mark walked silently to the car. Without asking, Mark pointed the jaguar south and flew down two-lane roads. Bella didn't feel purged until they had driven at least forty miles away. Mark drove with a hardened face for another twenty miles. He pulled into the driveway of a single-story brick house set far back from the road with a For Sale sign dangling from one hinge and stopped. Fallen leaves covered dead grass and did nothing for the property's curb appeal.

His face relaxed, and he looked at Bella. "I feel better. How about you?"

She nodded. She couldn't speak.

He offered a bottle of water to her, but Bella declined. He took a few sips himself. "Let's take a walk," he said. "The house looks vacant. Let's try the driveway and hope we don't get shot."

Bella almost laughed before she realized it was entirely possible for a homeowner in a rural area to have a shotgun at the ready for trespassers. She was safe, but she didn't want Mark in harm's way.

"Are you sure?" she asked.

He shrugged. "We're potential purchasers trying to get a closer look before calling the realtor."

They walked up the long drive without incident. There were no signs of life. No cars, bikes, or ATVs. No garbage can in the rack by the garage. A rusted mailbox lay on its side on the brick front porch. They sat on the steps.

"I was surprised," Bella said. "I didn't see that coming."

"No way did I expect him to say there was an unwritten policy to ignore patients in any condition on the night shift. Out of control. Sick. Seizing."

"Do you think we need to confirm the woman he replaced was fired for calling a doctor?" Bella asked. "Opal can easily find her name and current job."

"No," Mark said. "Cox believed that's why she was fired. He didn't have to be correct in that belief. We don't want to get sidetracked."

She'd taught him well. He was focused. He was looking at the end game and how to get there most directly.

Bella put her hand on Mark's. "We've got to see that tape. Yarbrough's prosecution was based on surveillance that showed him fixated on Evan Cooper's room. There was nothing about Yarbrough going into the rooms of other patients. I wonder if anyone else was hurt. He could have hit or choked other patients. Nothing was in the transcript about the condition of other patients on the ward. They might have had bruises or contusions or worse."

Mark exhaled slowly. "I'll reach out to my friend on the Petersburg PD. I'll get the warrant when we get back even if I have to go to Judge King's house. My friend can execute it first thing tomorrow morning before anyone knows about it. Once we have it, we can see for ourselves what went down that night."

He shook his head in disgust.

Bella squeezed his hand. "Mark, you're doing a great job. Evan Cooper's family is being represented by the best. You'll win big for them. You don't have to take on all the fallout. Let someone else put together a class action for all patients in the hospital that night. Someone else can investigate corruption in the Dinwiddie County prosecutor's office. The United State Attorney's office can bring criminal charges against the state for their role in Evan Cooper's murder. Someone else can appeal Yarbrough's conviction. It's not all on you. We're almost there."

He raised her hand and kissed it. He held it on the walk back to the car.

CHAPTER
FORTY-FIVE

All Hallows' Eve

There were only two people left on the list of homeless ghosts. Big had found resting places for the fifteen souls who remained after the first meeting. Bella and Big met to discuss their final plan.

"How are you holding up?" Bella asked.

"Good. Once you gave me the current locations I needed, it wasn't difficult to get the souls there. All were happy, or at least at peace. Having locations for the family cemeteries for those who couldn't go back helped. Three nineteenth century women had trouble understanding that an airport or cineplex or subdivision now sat on the site of their family farm. Taking them to cemeteries where their families were buried was the next best thing. One found her parents and the other two found their husbands and children."

"I'm so pleased. It's heartbreaking how they were treated. They were never told anything about the people they loved."

They both bowed their heads.

"Let's see what we can do for the remaining two," Bella said. "Who are they?"

"Mary is a thirteen-year-old girl who died from an epileptic seizure in 1915. When her parents discovered she had epilepsy at age eight, they committed her and never looked back.

"The young man—Bobby—died in a knife fight that broke out on his ward in 1959. He was twenty and had been here for two years. He and his girlfriend from the right side of the tracks eloped and were married in North Carolina. The girlfriend's father tracked them down, had the marriage annulled, and had Bobby committed as an undesirable. Bobby said the girlfriend sent him a letter saying she'd been wrong to marry him and was glad her father had made her see reason. She said she was marrying the heir to a pharmaceutical company. Bobby still wants her back."

Sad. Such sad stories. Bella thought Bobby would be the easiest to help. "He would be in his late seventies had he lived in human form. If the girlfriend was about the same age, she's probably still alive. Does he know the name of the man she married?"

"Maybe. He was just told an heir to a fortune. Bobby had an idea which fortune it was. He knew who the father had in mind for his girlfriend."

"Don't you think the girlfriend wrote the letter under duress if she wrote it at all?"

"Probably. Bobby never saw the letter. One of the nurses read it to him."

"And Bobby's literate?" Bella asked.

"Yes," Big said. "He wouldn't have needed anyone to read it to him."

"That means the girlfriend never had anything to do with it," Bella surmised. "The father most likely paid someone to read him a Dear John letter." Young love. Broken love. "Where did Bobby live?"

"Richmond."

"Well, there are only about half a dozen pharmaceutical fortunes here. If he can narrow it down to a last name, we can go from there. Intuition tells me the girlfriend never married. Get her last name too."

"And Mary?" he asked gently.

"Siblings? Cousins? Aunts? Uncles?"

"No siblings. First names only for the rest."

"I wonder if the parents were in agreement about institutionalizing her," Bella mused.

"You mean the husband dropped off Mary without telling the mother?"

"Or vice versa. The mother could have done it and told the father Mary ran away." She closed her eyes to think. "Let's start there. What has Mary said about her parents? Was she afraid of one or both of them?"

"She said her mother used to tell her she was an embarrassment. She never mentioned the father."

"Is there anywhere Mary wants to go? Or anything she wants? At eight, she probably wanted a pony unless she grew up on a farm. Where did she live?"

"Roanoke. She liked school and liked to read."

"I'll check on the parents' descendants and see if there is any possibility of a reunion. If not, I think near the Roanoke public library might be good."

They embraced. "We're almost there," Bella said.

Big held her in his arms for a long time. "I can't believe it. Finally."

CHAPTER
FORTY-SIX

November

Bella couldn't wait. She'd denied herself Daniel too long. She wanted to see him, feel his familiar body, and inhale the smell of him. Her need had intensified after the weekend in Bermuda with Mark. He was a good, sexy guy. He wasn't her Daniel.

She knew Daniel kept a rigid schedule. He was always in bed by eleven o'clock and up at eight. He ate breakfast and then took a walk with an aging Ivan, the chocolate lab/boxer mix dog he'd adopted along with a grey tabby cat named Holly from the animal rescue center before he was admitted to Commonwealth Psych. He ate lunch at noon, ran in the late afternoon about four, and ate dinner at seven. He walked Ivan again before bed.

Bella suspected Daniel took something to make him sleep. A dreamless, restful sleep but not terribly restorative. That was in her favor. He'd never know she was there.

She went to him the night after the deposition with Jess Cox, who'd been on duty the night Evan Cooper was murdered. His revelations about the specific instructions not to call security or a physician during the night were surprising and alarming. She now knew how close Daniel had come to being Larry Yarbrough's victim. That terrified her.

Daniel slept on his left side facing away from the window. Ivan snored at his feet. Bella slipped in through the window and lay on her side behind Daniel. Ivan stirred, but didn't wake. Spooning with Daniel was better than making love with anyone else alive. She felt his sweetness, his sadness, and his unfailing spirit when she rested her head on his shoulder. He didn't move all night. She lay there feeling comforted and whole. Soon. Soon, they would be together.

Daniel's sleep was that of synthetic stuff. Chemicals, binders, and dyes sprinkled quiet on his nerves, muscles, and brain. He reposed for eight hours. The drug's effect was predictable. Exactly eight hours after taking it, Daniel woke.

After the first night when she sought assurance that Daniel had survived Yarbrough's rampage, Bella spent every night with Daniel. Holding him calmed her. She believed she brought a certain peacefulness to Daniel. His breathing seemed more even when she left than when she arrived.

Ivan noticed her a few times. He, like other creatures, knew her ghostly form was benign. At most, his eyes would open, he'd look into her eyes, and he'd go back to sleep. Ivan looked old and tired. Bella believed Ivan was holding on to protect Daniel and wooing him to be well.

One morning, Bella lingered. She left long enough for Daniel to wake, shower, and dress, but she returned to his room, where she overheard his conversation with Selma in the kitchen.

"We'll leave at nine for your appointment, okay?"

"Sure, Mom."

Bella heard the clatter of silverware and smelled the rich aroma of coffee. Coffee was something she missed. Coffee, chocolate, and champagne. If she could take those along with Daniel, eternity would be more than blissful.

"Daniel, you're looking better in the past few days. Any secrets you want to share?" Selma asked.

"I've been sleeping really well. I feel like I have a heat source in the small of my back that makes me relax. I almost dream, or I dream for seconds. Maybe I'm getting acclimated to the sleep medication. I wake up feeling better than I used to, but I don't feel any sluggish effects."

"Good," Selma said. "That new medication is working. You're improving. Maybe you should mention that to the doctor today."

Bella was pleased she had such a beneficial effect on Daniel. He could mention it to the psychiatrist, but he wouldn't be able to explain that it was the bond between the two of them and not just some chemical improving his sleep.

CHAPTER
FORTY-SEVEN

"This is abominable," Bella said. She was furious. She stood with Mark in front of a VCR Opal had acquired and watched the original unedited hospital surveillance tape from the night of Evan Cooper's murder. "I can't believe someone would be so cruel. Everything Larry Yarbrough said was true. He was out of his mind on bath salts, desperate to cool down, and ran into Evan's room repeatedly making a terrible racket."

Worse, Evan Cooper's screams were audible.

Jess Cox, who sat in the bulletproof nursing station, did nothing. He didn't respond to anything Yarbrough did or Cooper's screams that turned to gagging. Yarbrough had torn off his clothes and run with purpose through the ward, screaming and cursing and begging for cool air. He pummeled the glass shield, threw a chair at it, and pelted it with bottles of medicine from the first aid cabinet he ripped off the wall. Iodine, cough syrup, and pink

265

Pepto-Bismol splattered on and down the window. Cox yelled for Yarbrough to shut up. Yarbrough ran in and out of every patient's room at least twice. The tape was six hours of nonstop belligerence and hysteria. And death.

"I've seen enough," Bella said at the three-hour point. "I'll draft a search warrant for the Dinwiddie County prosecutor's home and office."

She went into the conference room and closed the door. She paced around the conference table. She wanted to punch someone. She never expected to discover so much indifference to human suffering by someone charged with at least doing no harm.

This would end their case. Bella was certain when the computers at the prosecutor's home and office were examined, evidence of tampering the tape would be obvious. Not only was the tape six hours long instead of twenty-five minutes, it included audio as well as visual tracks. No doubt software used to separate the two would be found on one of the prosecutor's computers.

Prosecutorial misconduct aside, the newly discovered evidence would make it clear that the hospital staff knew what Yarbrough was doing and failed to call for security or medical assistance. That willful blindness established the state's legal culpability in the death of Evan Cooper.

Mark could handle the rest of the case. The search warrant for the prosecutor's computers, the Motion for Summary Judgment, and a final argument were complete. Mark was on the phone when Bella entered his office. She wordlessly handed the USB drive to Mark. Mark mouthed,

"See you later," as she left. Outside, relief surged through her. One part of her mission was finished. She didn't feel even a twinge of regret for deserting Mark.

CHAPTER
FORTY-EIGHT

Thanksgiving Eve

"You're certain everyone's out?" Bella asked. She'd stopped in the pharmacy to get exactly what she needed before meeting Big. "Checked every room myself, including offices. The bomb threat is being treated as real. Everyone's out."

The two worked their way from the third floor to the basement, pouring gasoline along the corridors and lighting matches. They threw in oxygen tanks as they found them. By the time they reached the basement, there was a satisfying blaze going above them. The soundtrack was crackles from burning wood, great groans from falling beams, and blasts from explosions of equipment. Thunderous smoke clouded everything.

They raced out to see EMS crews calling individual patient names. The teams had warrants to seize patients and transfer them to specific approved locations. That was going smoothly except for one man in a suit who was trying to get an EMS driver to take him off the premises. Bella ran to him and pulled him back by his suit jacket. When he turned around, he saw nothing. She saw the hospital's chief of staff trying to get away rather than oversee the care of his patients.

Infuriated, Bella grabbed the doctor's hand and pulled him down the gravel driveway away from the action. She withdrew the scalpel from her pocket and repeatedly sliced him in the stomach and slashed his face and arms. She made herself visible.

"Who are you?" he huffed, panting and bleeding.

"Someone whose lover and daughter spent time in this hellhole. They could have died for no reason because you weren't providing the most basic kind of care. You're not a disgrace. You're evil."

She kept slashing him. Bella didn't want to kill him. She wanted him to suffer. His screams brought no attention to him. Patients were priority for EMS. When she had emptied her rage, Bella flung the doctor aside and walked away.

***

The twosome sat on the grass well away from the scene. The building had collapsed in some sections, but the fire was controlled.

"I can't believe we did it," Bella said. Tears poured down her face. "It's over. All that horror is over."

Big hugged her. "It is. It's really over."

She stayed in his arms and cried like a child

whose fondest wish had come true. He held her tightly. When she finished, she sat up and looked at him. "What's next for you?"

"I'm going back to Potts Mountain to find my children if they're alive. If not, I'll lay myself down beside my wife. I'm going home."

Bella nodded.

"And you?"

Before she could answer, there was a shout. "Big," called a man about her age as he ran up and threw his arms around her collaborator. Big held him close.

"What's going on?" the man asked.

"It's almost gone." Big put his arm around the man's shoulders. "Patients have been evacuated, ghosts have been sent to their rightful places, and this hospital of horrors is burning to the ground."

The man stood there, amazed and speechless, before Big made introductions.

"Gregg, this is Bella. She's my accomplice in destroying this place.

"Bella, this is Gregg. He…"

"LouLou's Gregg?" she asked.

"Yes." Big nodded with a smile.

"Did you come back for her? For LouLou?" she asked.

"Yes. I tried and tried and this is where I broke through. I don't know how to get to her from here."

"Do you love her?" Bella searched his face.

"With all my being."

LouLou had paid for hurting Daniel. Maybe not enough, but Bella and Daniel would soon be beyond this realm. LouLou was wretched alone. Gregg had come from the other side of the globe to be with LouLou. Bella couldn't deny them happiness. It was too cruel. She grabbed Gregg's hand. "I know how to get there. I'll take you to her."

She blew Big a kiss. He smiled and waved and then he was gone. Bella held Gregg's hand tightly as she willed them to LouLou's loft.

CHAPTER
FORTY-NINE

The network's best local reporter stood away from the scene of the fire, but it could be seen in the background.

"The fire that started about nine twenty-five this morning in which no lives were lost marked the end of what has been a turbulent time for Commonwealth Psychiatric Hospital. Yesterday, Federal Judge Madeline King granted Summary Judgment against the state for its role in the death of Evan Cooper three years ago.

"She awarded the plaintiffs sixty million dollars in damages, which is treble what was asked, and ordered the immediate closing of the hospital according to a plan based on individual patients' diagnosis, age, and gender. Warrants to transfer every patient were being executed when a bomb threat was called in to the hospital.

"The threat caused evacuation of the building. EMS teams responding to the scene transferred patients according to the warrants signed by Judge King. The hospital's chief of staff, whose name has not been released, suffered injuries and was arrested along with other key staff as accomplices in the murder of Evan Cooper.

"This follows the arrest at dawn of the prosecutor from Dinwiddie County who led the case against another patient, Larry Yarbrough, for the murder of Evan Cooper. The prosecutor is charged with tampering with evidence and obstruction of justice. He's believed to have edited the six-hour surveillance video from the hospital cameras on the night of the murder down to twenty-five minutes and deleted the audio portion.

"Sources close to the arrest say the missing hours show hospital staff allowing Mr. Yarbrough to rampage through the ward and in the rooms of other patients without restraint while high on bath salts. Bath salts, the name for a lethal combination of synthetic drugs, is known to trigger violent outbursts over a period of several days. Mr. Yarbrough was convicted of second degree murder and died in custody last month. The cause of death was cardiac and liver failure due to prolonged use of bath salts.

"The attorney representing Evan Cooper's family in its case against the state is Mark Hoffman. Our network's chief legal correspondent has a live interview with him coming up. The state's attorney general has made no remarks."

***

Bella watched the television coverage in Roy's diner near LouLou's loft. She was invisible and didn't detect any Sensitives nearby. She was pleased LouLou had been reunited with Gregg. He seemed ecstatic that she'd been able to take him to his beloved LouLou. She didn't know how long Gregg would be able to stay in this realm with LouLou, but it wasn't her concern. She'd reunited them. The two of them would make choices that worked for them.

She hadn't seen Mark since the day they'd watched the surveillance video. She'd made an invisible visit long enough to make sure Mark realized her departure was permanent. Mark hadn't noticed until late afternoon, when Opal entered his office with the phone Bella left behind from the genius phone system. She no longer needed it.

"What's this?" Mark asked.

"Bella's phone. It must have fallen out of her bag. She's too meticulous to forget it."

Opal asked if there was anything else for her to do and when Mark said no, she left. Mark continued to review the Motion for Summary Judgment he intended to file the next day. When he hit sleep and the computer screen went dark, he picked up Bella's phone.

"I'm going to give her a hard time about losing this when she comes in tomorrow," he said aloud. "Finally, a mistake by Ms. Brilliant and Gorgeous." His eyes crinkled with mischief. Before he put it down, he saw there was a text addressed to him. He opened it, read it, and pushed his chair back away from the desk.

Kick Ass.

Those two words were all the notice she left. She watched as it dawned on him that the message meant she wasn't coming back. He loosened his tie, made himself a scotch, and when he sat on the white sofa, closed his eyes. She saw he was fighting tears. He finally let them flow. He looked heartbroken, but there was no one to see him.

She knew she should feel something, but all that came to her was relief. Mark was a changed man. He'd finished the trial with bravado and a win for the Coopers and his loyal three-member team. Eventually, he'd realize she'd just been an eye-opener for him. Bella hoped he'd take a long vacation after the case was won, find a woman to love, and live happily ever after in some place other than Richmond. Maybe his sister in Australia had a friend who would appreciate and love him. At least Mark now knew there were possibilities in his life that he shouldn't waste. She'd given him that and he'd served as her human conduit for justice. Bella considered it a fair exchange.

CHAPTER FIFTY

Daniel sat in the armchair in his bedroom sobbing with his face in his hands. Surely, he wouldn't be upset at news reports of the finale of Commonwealth Psychiatric Hospital.

"Daniel," Bella said softly as she approached him. "Daniel, what's wrong?"

"Ivan died," he mumbled with his hands still covering his face.

"I'm so sorry. When?"

"This morning, I woke up and he was there." He pointed to the foot of the bed. "He must have died in the night."

She sank to her knees in front of Daniel and put her head in his lap. Bella had spent the night on the grounds of Commonwealth Psych to start the fire as soon as Big gave her a signal. She hadn't slept with Daniel so she hadn't seen Ivan. Maybe he understood Bella was coming for Daniel and his job was done.

"The vet just left with him. He had kidney disease. I gave him the pills every day, but I guess he just finally wore out. He was old."

When he stopped sobbing, Daniel realized who was with him. "Bella?"

"Yes, Daniel, it's me."

He pulled her onto his lap and cried into her neck. She held him and stroked his hair and murmured nonsense to calm him. He clung to her.

"Bella, they told me you were dead, that it was impossible for us to have had an affair. The police, my lawyer, Rob. Everyone said you were dead."

"Daniel, I don't live in human form anymore. It doesn't mean I don't exist. I'm here for you. For us."

He held her tightly and continued to cry softly. Finally, he sat back and wiped his eyes with the back of his hand.

"I went to a paranormal specialist. He said you and I had been together because of what he called our extraordinary bond. He said our love knew no bounds. He was the only person who believed me."

She kissed him. "He was right. I'm sorry no one else understood."

He sat silently, content to hold her. When he did speak, it was through tears. "Bella, why didn't you tell me about our child?" His brown eyes were rimmed with sadness.

"I couldn't tell you in a letter. I wanted you to come to Paris. I was afraid to fly while pregnant. I didn't know anything about pregnancy, really." She paused. "I didn't want you to be with me because of the baby. I wanted you to want me and us. If you didn't, then I wasn't going to play the pregnancy card."

"I did want you. You know that. We talked about

it that year when we were together. Before my father died. I was just depressed and stubborn and proud."

"Shhhh," she whispered. "It doesn't matter. We're together now."

"You were alone and pregnant."

"I had friends from the Sorbonne. I met the Flemings through the adoption agency while I was pregnant. They were nice people and wanted LouLou very much. I couldn't keep her without you."

"I'm sorry. I was such a fool."

"We're together now. LouLou is as happy and healthy as her illness allows her to be. The Fleming family adores her. Gregg, the man who loves her, returned to her today. They're happy."

"That's all that matters," he said.

***

Their lovemaking was languorous, sensuous, and rapturous. They took time to appreciate the bodies each knew so well. Bella closed her eyes and luxuriated in the feel of Daniel, his touch, his mouth on hers. She felt like she was seventeen again.

Daniel lay on his back and pulled her close. "We're back in a single bed. Where we started."

"Are we?" She smiled as she looked into his eyes and held his face in her hands.

"Time drops away when I'm with you. I feel whole. Please, never leave me," he pleaded.

He was ready.

"Daniel," she whispered. "It's time."

278

"Now?" He immediately understood.

"I came back for you. I came back to close that psychiatric hospital and I did. It burned to the ground this morning. The patients are safe and the ghosts have homes."

"I can come with you now?" he repeated. She watched him struggle to understand.

"Yes. Only if you want to come."

"I don't want to be without you ever. Where will we go?"

"Anywhere you want."

He spoke through tears. "I'd like to go to St. John where we swam, made love, and slept in a hammock between coconut trees under the stars. That was where we were happiest, I think."

"I was happy wherever I was with you, but I think St. John is the best choice." He continued to cry. "Bella, I'm tired. I hate Mørk. I used to accept it. Then I disliked it. Now, I despise it. It runs my life. I want nothing more than to be free with you."

He looked down at her. "You are the most beautiful woman in any universe, Bella. I've always loved you and will through eternity."

Everything had been worthwhile just to hear him say those words.

CHAPTER
FIFTY-ONE

"You really want to do this?" she asked softly as she sat upright.

He nodded.

"Then we must plan. Where do you want to leave?"

"Here, in his room with you." He held her hand.

They discussed details. Bella brought morphine she'd grabbed from the hospital pharmacy. Daniel would take pills so it would look like suicide. The family would probably think the loss of Ivan triggered it.

Daniel didn't want his mother to be the one to find him. He sent a text to Rob asking that he stop by in three hours to pick up something for Thanksgiving dinner the next day. Rob had a key to the villa.

"One last thing for Rob to do for me. He must be as tired as I am. He's run two households, parented Kate on my behalf, and looked after me for too long. I owe him a lot."

"I'm sure he doesn't mind. He loves you, Daniel. By pure grace, he's not the one who lives with Mørk."

"Do you think so?"

"Of course, Daniel. Your dad is a Sensitive. You have Mørk. Both your children have a mental illness. Neither Rob nor either of his sons inherited anything."

"I never thought of it that way. You make me see things differently, Bella. You always have." She kissed him. "I want to write Mom a note. Just to tell her I'm happy. She'll be free of taking care of me."

Daniel opened his top dresser drawer and pulled out a black and white composition book. He tore a page out and wrote in block letters, "Please don't be sad. I'm free. I love you, Mom. Thank you." He folded it and gave it to Bella. "Could you put it in her bedroom? On her nightstand. I'm going to make a drink and toast Ivan."

Bella quickly pulled the blue wrap dress around her and took the note to Selma's room. When she returned, Daniel was dressed and sitting on the bed holding an empty tumbler of scotch. He had gotten all of his pills out of their containers. "I just got them refilled so I have a lot. I want another drink too."

She watched as he poured a second drink. He patted the bed next to him. "Be with me."

She sat next to him and held his hand in silence. When he was ready, Daniel swallowed a handful of pills, washed them down with scotch, and lay on the bed. Bella gave him a shot that would kill him. She didn't want to depend upon mistakes in dosage, time, or interruptions. She curled into him.

"I love you, Daniel, with all my heart."

He put his arms around her. "I love you always," he said as he drifted off to sleep, "Bella."

About the Author

Born in Venice, Italy, Adam Zorzi is the author of Blind Spot, Blind Trust, and Blind Rage that comprise the Blind Justice Trilogy. He lives in New York.

Facebook:
https://www.facebook.com/profile.php?id=1
00012263627516&fref=ts

Blind Justice Trilogy Facebook Page:
https://www.facebook.com/BlindJusticeTril
ogyAdamZorzi/?fref=ts

Twitter:
https://twitter.com/adamzorzi

Website:
http://www.adamzorzi.com/